In the Name
of Desire

T0051393

SUNDIAL HOUSE

SUNDIAL HOUSE EDITORIAL BOARD

Anne Freeland
J. Bret Maney
Alberto Medina
Graciela Montaldo
João Nemi Neto
Rachel Price
Eunice Rodríguez Ferguson
Kirmen Uribe

In the Name
of Desire

João Sivério Trevisan

Translated by

Ben de Witte & João Nemi Neto

SUNDIAL HOUSE

**SUNDIAL
HOUSE**
New York ♦ Philadelphia

Copyright © 2023 João Silvério Trevisan

Copyright © 2023 Ben De Witte and João Nemi Neto

Published by arrangement with Agência Literária Riff,
Rio de Janeiro, Brazil.

This is a work of fiction. Names, characters, places, and incidents
either are the product of the author's imagination or are used
fictitiously. Any resemblance to actual persons, living or dead,
events, or locales is entirely coincidental.

All rights reserved. No part of this book may be reproduced or used
in any manner without written permission of the copyright owners,
except for the use of quotations in a book review.

Second paperback edition: October 2023

Book design by Lisa Hamm

Floorplan illustration by Tom Breslin

Proofreading by Anne Freeland

ISBN: 979-8-9879264-1-3

Contents

Introduction

BEN DE WITTE AND JOÃO NEMI NETO

MULTIFACETED WRITER, cinematographer, activist and cultural critic João Silverio Trevisan (1944) wrote his third novel *Em nome do desejo* in the early 1980s. It was published in 1983 in Brazil and came out around the same time that—what we now call—LGBTQAI+ rights were, so to speak, having their first national "coming out." The country's military dictatorship was living through its last moments, and the first homosexual liberation group *Somos* (literally "we are" or "we exist"), of which Trevisan was a founding member, had formed a couple of years before. This historical timing, in which homosexuality became increasingly visible to the national audience, coincided with the coming of the AIDS crisis, which in the public opinion would often cast homosexual visibility in a less than favorable light. This may in part explain the generally lukewarm reactions to Trevisan's novel, which unapologetically presents a homoerotic content against the background of a tightly run Catholic seminary. The book brings to the front dissident sexualities, while at the same time describing the terrors of growing up in a seminary—up till recently in Brazil a common manner for poor families to guarantee an education for their children: the Catholic church offered to educate their children in exchange for them becoming priests later.

Em nome do desejo is told by a first-person narrator, who as a true memorialist minutely recounts some of the key moments in his formative years at a Catholic seminary on the countryside of Brazil in the 1950s. At the time of the release, critics were confused with the tone of the novel. While pitched by the publisher as a *romance*, many critics could not pinpoint whether the text was meant to be read as fiction, or was in fact a memoir. This confusion seems deliberate on part of the novel's design; while it is tempting to label the text as a memoir, its manner of narration defers a too straightforward conclusion. While the narrator confidently addresses the reader in the first person at the beginning of the book, the story gradually switches to a more impersonal form of narration, but again resumes explicitly in the first person at the very end. In the Portuguese original, for instance, the narrator occasionally refrains from attributing a clear subject or agent to "a memória" (the memory), precisely when the reader might expect a self-conscious claiming of a particular memory by the narrator (i.e., as "minha memória," or *my* memory). Memory in these instances seems to play a game on us, or maybe even on the narrator himself. This subtle distancing effect can nowadays be appreciated as an attempt to blur too neat a distinction between fact and fiction. The blurring of elements of reality, memory, and past are at the heart of what is now often called "autofiction"; the author only tentatively assumes the part a first person-narrator, giving to the reader possible elements of his own life that are richly intertwined with a haze of magic.

The unsettling, wavering subjectivity in narration is not the only aspect that makes *Em nome do desejo* an intriguing read. Several stylistic and cultural particularities give this novel a remarkable tone and flavor. Trevisan's frequent use of unusually long sentences, strung together in a peculiar rhythm with copious punctuation, are challenging not only for translators, but also for readers of Portuguese. The book's syntax and style suit the author's liking for elaborate description, sometimes lavish and varied, otherwise repetitive and almost deliberately matter-of- factual. This manner of writing seems carefully calculated; the book's prose incorporates a necessarily wide register of references (most clearly and abundantly to Catholicism, but also to literary tradition, music, film, popular culture, specific foods, tastes and local customs) to appropriately scale up and down between the earthly and the divine. That is perhaps where desire happens in this novel; through the mill of words, thoughts, imageries and gestures, but always intransigently.

The novel resolutely amalgamates the mundane and the religious, striving to understand and transcend the mystery of love and desire. Accordingly, the narrator mimes the ritualistic language of the Roman Catechism, though ultimately, at the story's ending, only to declare its impotence.

Faced with these stylistic and thematic particularities, the translators have sought to find a balance between literal "faithfulness" and what seemed feasible. In an age in which the work of translation is often scrutinized for traces of the "translator's voice," we recognize that *In the Name of Desire* walks a tightrope between the demands of the original and its intended new readership. We hope that our translation choices did justice to *Em nome do desejo*, and that *In the Name of Desire* will bring novel appreciation to its ingenious author. We thank João Silvério Trevisan for his trust, as well as Columbia University for supporting the Sundial House series. Special thanks to Eunice Rodríguez Ferguson for her boundless enthusiasm and support of this initiative, and to Anne Freeland for her insightful feedback and her keen editorial eye.

In the Name
of Desire

pigsty chickencoop

vegetable garden

chapel

SLOPING TERRAIN

shoe storage

athletic wardrobe closet (basements)

storage

stairs

LOWER RECESS

guestroom (underground)

bathroom for older students

wardrobe for older students

Rector's room

classroom

infirmary for older students

older students dormitory

classroom

kitchen (underground)

study hall for older students

Rector's office

front desk

study hall for younger students

dining hall (underground)

courtyard

central corridor

library

BACK WALLS

nuns' house (underground)

bathroom for younger students

infirmary for younger students

younger students dormitory

classroom

wardrobe for younger students

spiritual director's room

classroom

FRONT WALLS

ball closet (basement)

arcade

storage (basement)

stairs

SLOPING TERRAIN

UPPER RECESS

eucalyptus grove

eucalyptus grove

soccer field

recess shed

arcade

eucalyptus grove

eucalyptus grove

This is passion according to Spinoza:
desire (the effort to persevere in being)
is not defined as merely another passion,
but rather as the condition of all passions.
Simply because it is desire itself
that elaborates them in the imagination.
Hence, the soul does not suffer passion.
To Spinoza, the soul is entirely passion.
—from the diary of Jean-Paul Carraldo

Are you a Christian?
No. I am brave, I am strong.
I am a son of Death.
—Oswald de Andrade

There are boys and girls who at the start of adolescence
see themselves loving against the tides.
Even though they are perplexed, they do love.
This book wants to honor their audacity.

Overture

I SEE myself entering the dark, like someone penetrating a sanctuary, anxious to find a light. When I turn on the lamp on the side table, I am startled. In front of me stands a singular vase in the shape of a human skull that contains fresh white lilies. For some time, I consider this coincidence that I know is not a coincidence. I place the suitcase on the chair. I take off my jacket. I take a deep breath. I realize that I am tired from this long journey. I'm trying to get used to the monastic austerity of the guest room, which looks the same in all houses of religion. A crucifix on the wall above the small table, a single bed with white sheets, and a nightstand on which, of course, lies a copy of the Bible. It immediately occurs to me that the Bible will keep good company to the two Spanish mystics whose poems I carry in my luggage. Because of the yellowish light I can't tell the exact color of the wall. Back then the lights of the day were weak in this part of the city. That is why, when I parked the car outside next to the gates, my initial impression of the manor seemed a little macabre. Shadows spread over the exposed brick walls, shadows surrounding the fig tree lane, shadows hiding the entrance that I remembered as imposing and rotund. Only after I crossed the lane did I realize that nothing had changed in the old manor. As expected, the ocher bricks looked more faded. The architectural lines that sought to imitate a sacred style remained untouched by time. In the shadows I start to discern familiar signs.

And now I wonder for what reasons I wanted to go back.

There is an old French film in which the character patiently visits each of his friends and favorite places to say goodbye. In the end, he shoots himself in the face. Yes, apparently tragedies happen only in films. Even though there are people dying among us every day and every second, we more consciously envision pain in the realm of fiction. Many experience life as a space for mediocrities that are tolerable for some, or insupportable for others. Perhaps because I felt oversaturated, I decided to return to this house where I had lived the most intense years of my life. I decided that I should. I called an influential former colleague in the city and asked him to find me a bed here, for one night. Only then did I learn that the old manor had long ago been transformed into an orphanage. The dorms must now be populated by dozens of lost children. Perhaps the environment hasn't changed that much.

❖ ❖ ❖

I feel some kind of suppressed nostalgia. Who knows what I hope to find here? Perhaps a sacred space, deep within me, that sometimes looks like a mirage. Still, there is always the possibility of discovering some treasure, buried in my forty years of age. One inevitably thinks of the wife of Lot, who became a statue of salt when she looked back. I came here to take the same risk. What might be down there, on the bottom, underneath the smoke?

❖ ❖ ❖

I contemplate this very singular skull, which looks all the more macabre due to the flowers that serve as its crown. Why are there always human skulls in sacred places? They say that in the Mayan ruins lies an arena with walls of human skulls carved in low reliefs that depict sacrifices to the God of Death. I now look at this skull as if standing in front of a mirror.

❖ ❖ ❖

What will I say to this manifestation of death that beholds me? I will say that I am a victim of the absence of pain. Throughout all these years I have been learning to overcome suffering, and today I am able to smile as if for a toothpaste ad. Yesterday I got drunk, once more. I have no idea where I spent the night. In a nightclub, in a motel, in a massage parlor? In the morning I made a phone call and got into the car. On the road I was almost euphoric. I only stopped in front of the gates of this manor, where I vaguely sensed that I was looking for a primordial element.

Looking back, I see myself more or less like this: I grew up, I studied and pursued a field of expertise, got married and had children, drank beer in countless places in the city, and I punched my card every morning in one place.

This skull speaks to me of radical things. Possibly memories of an age-old radicalism. Unhinged mystics who went into caves to contemplate the face of God. Nowadays people hardly talk of the Carthusian order that was founded by some saint. In which century? But they still talk of John of the Cross and Teresa of Ávila, also known as *Terezona*, Big Teresa. Unsettled saints whose heavenly visions made them rise into air for an impossible love. Are their lost verses not fixed to my memory? Why?

❖ ❖ ❖

"Why do you wound my heart
And then refuse to heal?
And since you took it from me,
Why do you leave it now,
Abandoning the thing you robbed?"
—St. John of the Cross[1]

❖ ❖ ❖

No. I stopped believing in such crazy dreams long ago. I have missed you for a long time.

God, how can one find so much love again?

❖ ❖ ❖

Yes, I acknowledge that I attempted to escape. I cannot sleep. I renounce the manor's old peacefulness. Strange sen-

---

1 All translations of the poems of St. John of the Cross are by Professor Willis Barnstone. (Barnstone, Willis. *The Poems of St. John of the Cross,* translated by Barnstone, New Directions, 1972.)

sations invade me in this place that is inhabited by my old ghosts. Who is there, forcing my door?

Almost thirty years ago I lived here. Now I return to the origins. What do I seek? The skull replies: to solve a mystery.

A thought occurs to me, looking into the hollow eyes of the skull: how obscene, that life is killed by the very will to survive.

I fear that life and passion are enemies. If there is a danger to falling in love, it is because in it life feels threatened. Paradoxes that no drunken good cheer ever solved.

Yet is there not too much complexity in the underground of everyday life? Would a messy chunk of life not be deserving of reverence, precisely because of the passion suffocated in it?

❖ ❖ ❖

Mindlessly, I unveil my belly in front of the crowned skull. There is no shyness on my part. How much alcohol did it take to forge (and preserve) this respectable appearance that I now contemplate through the skull?

❖ ❖ ❖

Could this manor have remained the same?

❖ ❖ ❖

I think hard and don't know if the arrangement of the rooms has changed over time. Four classrooms, two on each side of the main entrance. To the left, the library. On the right, the entrance for visitors, and, behind it, the rectory. The central corridor crosses the building from side to side and connects the external courtyard (on the left) to the chapel (on the right). Further on, on the left, the dormitory of the younger students (where the sun hits in the morning), with the spiritual director's room in the corner; on the right, the dormitory of the older students (where the sun hits in the afternoon), adjacent to the rector's room. Crossing the large dormitories, on one side were the wardrobes, lavatories, and infirmary for the younger students. On the other side were the wardrobes, lavatories, and infirmary for the older students. Between the lavatories, on each side, lay the study halls of the older ones and younger ones, interconnected by a single door that was rarely opened, so as not to allow what were called dangerous combinations. Because the land descended on a steep slope, there were cellars from the bedrooms onwards, the first ones built rather low and used to store assorted odds and ends on both sides of the building. Further on, however, the cellars were sufficiently tall and better suited for their intended use. Underneath the wardrobes there was storage space for shoes and sporting materials, respectively. And at the bottom of the ground floor of the house were the living quarters of the six nuns, the kitchen, and the common dining hall. The cafeteria stood in communication with the inner courtyard, which was surrounded by a false colonnade and opened on the left onto the outer courtyard, and in the front onto the central corridor. In the external courtyard, the same sequence of columns was reproduced, in order to accentuate the conventual atmosphere of the building, which was, in fact, too prosaic to achieve this style. At the back of the ground floor, on the right, to this day lie the guest rooms, one of which I am in now, almost completely cut off from the rest of the house. Here you can easily feel a sensation of total isolation. There is no noise from cars, which even during the day rarely reaches this suburb far from the city center. I hear only the wind in the trees. Ah, yes, the eucalyptus trees. On the left side of the grounds was the soccer field, surrounded by eucalyptus trees, whose familiar noise I even now still hear. To the right were the pigsty, the chicken coop, and the vegetable garden, just behind the chapel. And walls. In the front, the back, and on each side of the rectangular property, walls demarcating the borders with the world.

I contemplate the skull with lilies. Horrors, fears, panic. In these forty years I have let myself sink into a kind of quicksand, or maybe into a tank of warm and anesthetic alcohol.

When exactly did this need to suffocate desires and to claim what I learned to call the "sensible life" begin?

Insomnia. It would make no sense to hope that I could sleep when in fact I came here precisely to remember. Wide awake and perfectly at peace.

❖ ❖ ❖

I wonder, what is this thing that we call passion?

❖ ❖ ❖

I think I will find here minute recollections of passion. Precious ones.

❖ ❖ ❖

There is a boy at the beginning of everything. Intense memories of the times when I was simply called Tiquinho. I shudder. I feel traces of my volcanic center. I had almost forgotten. The truth is that I was piling up stones on this boy, and so Tiquinho ended up buried. I now find myself compelled to begin an archaeological excavation. Something is breathing inside me again. Penetrating perfumes.

❖ ❖ ❖

The skull is unrelenting. Its white lilies give off a smell that stuns me, and the passion has a strange name that I insist on obscuring. I pronounce your magic name. Teenage stuff, it was then said. I feel inclined to doubt now. There is a certain Abel. I try to pronounce his name.

❖ ❖ ❖

In front of this mirror, I hear voices. So many voices that I get confused. Young voices that are also in mutation: hoarse cockerels crows. Bell sounds. Whistles. Murmurs of sleepy prayers after lunch and before bed. Muffled cries in the middle of the night. Snoring. Weak moans. Wild screams.

❖ ❖ ❖

Then I contemplate myself in the mirror, floating before my eyes. At this time of night, I see that my eyes are blurred by an unsettling fog. I am a witness to my fear of being enveloped in poisonous gases, misshapen things from the past. I open my trunk of old, moldy fantasies. I choke with emotion at what I see.

❖ ❖ ❖

What really happened between Tiquinho and a certain Abel?—I hear myself asking the flowered skull. The question has mysterious implications. Will I be compelled to reconsider the very nature of mystery?

❖ ❖ ❖

Well now, crowned skull. I retrace my steps, coming and going through the room that my insomnia has transfigured. I am what was and what came. I see myself on the left. And on the right, my double, myself. I suffer tensions from outside, out of pure fear. Then I watch myself surrender. I see my hands joining in front of my face, and I can't resist surrendering to confession, sitting before this wise skull that has blossomed. Turning inward, I find myself thinking about the great human emotions. There are those who become ecstatic, as if looking at the world from atop a spaceship. Rare, enviable visions. There are those who, unmoved, observe the same distance when they are face to face with death. But they cannot recount those final, exceptional moments on the border between pain and nothingness. Their secret dies with them. This one however, standing with his head down in front of the skull (his mirror), safekeeps memories like a burnt diamond. I suspect that something is possessing him at dawn, and that he wants to confess what is going on inside. Suddenly, I sense an unknown euphoria inside him. I think that he convinced himself that, in his own way, he too had experienced great emotions. It is true: he is possessed. I see that our subject, narcotized by the specter of reason, wants to defy all prescriptions. Like a plump reptile he consents to plunge into the frightful seas of his revelatory insomnia. What courage for a reptile! He finally decides to redeem old carcasses. Or would it be a backward look, seeking to unravel those days' spectacle of fire and smoke? Well then, I see myself entering the private alcove of my passion. He who is contemplating the skull inlaid with lilies is not afraid to encounter statues of salt along the way. He is already hopelessly shrouded in fog. I follow his steps on this journey, or on this archeological expedition.

Of Obedience
and Other Mysteries

*Let's say that here we start with a radical plunge into the heart.
Are many mysteries kept in this well?*

In those days, the heart was truly a quilt made of pure
mysteries. And the mysteries together formed a drama,
because it was said that God directed everything.

As it is described in Isaiah 40, 22–23?

Yes. That God that "is he that sitteth upon the circle of
the earth, and the inhabitants thereof are as grasshoppers;
that stretcheth out the heavens as a curtain, and spreadeth
them out as a tent to dwell in: That bringeth the princes
to nothing; he maketh the judges of the earth as vanity."
Omnipotent and Uncompromising.

Every drama unfolds on a stage. What is the stage of those days?

The same place where I am now. Time: more than twenty-five years ago, almost thirty. And still it seems like it was
yesterday.

Who were the characters in this very ancient drama?

Boys and teenagers, between 10 and 15 years old, in total about sixty, who thought they were there to attend to a call from God to be his ministers and representatives.

Could any boy be a minister of God?

Yes, as long as he was chosen.

How could a boy know if he was elected?

By consulting the catechism that would say: when you feel you have the calling, when you are a friend of prayer, when you are pure and studious, and when you have good health. Or so it was, according to the dead letter, on paper. In practice these questions involved more nuanced distinctions. Many boys had a calling because of family pressure— either because their mother "had made a promise to give a son to the priesthood," or because the education for the chosen children was free of charge.

What other practical criteria informed the mission of being God's representative?

Since, in addition to being honorable, the mission of representing God on earth was arduous, these boys learned how to strictly interpret the role of being the Chosen Ones. After all, they would follow in the footsteps of God, who had made himself incarnate, suffered, and been crucified for the love of mankind. And loving mankind was a task not only difficult, but also dangerous—as will be seen. Precisely because of these dangers, the chosen were divided into two groups, according to age: the younger ones were from ten to thirteen years old; the older ones from thirteen onwards. The younger boys were more numerous. As they grew up, they often declined the divine call—sometimes not at all decorously: by being expelled, for example, on account of bad behavior. Hence the smaller number of older ones. This was considered normal: among the many that were called, only a few were chosen.

What was that place called, where the future representatives of God prepared themselves?

It was called Seminary. Hence the elect, who acted on this stage, were called seminarians.

It is assumed that every drama must have one or more protagonists. In this case, who would those be?

So as not to get too far ahead, for now I'll just say that the first protagonist was a sensitive and delicate boy, recently included in the group of the older ones, since he had just turned thirteen. His name to this day is João. At that time, he was sometimes called Joãozinho. But he was better known as Tico-Tico, because of his face full of freckles that called to mind the eponymous bird. From Tico-Tico the name then evolved to Tiquinho, since he was small—a little morsel of a boy. If my memory is not mistaken, he was shy, corroded by a passion that drove him to pursue endless love interests, and moved by an excessive honesty that frequently made him a victim of moral and spiritual scruples without end. The third year of middle school was about to begin, and that year his heart would live through an almost atomic bombardment of discoveries. As for the second protagonist, he was called Abel—Abel Rebebel, certainly a charming name. He enters the scene late, so I will only deal with him further on. For now, it is enough to say that Abel Rebebel was made to never be forgotten. That is why his importance goes beyond the bricks of these walls, vanquishes the inflexibility of time, and pierces the stones of the heart.

What is the intrigue of this drama?

Intrigue seems out of fashion nowadays. But as this story concerns bygone memories, the latest fashion doesn't really matter. It will suffice, therefore, to confess that there is indeed a kind of intrigue. Worse even: a love intrigue. Perhaps I will be saved from accusations of nostalgia by adding that the love affair is just a pretext to talk about the great passions of the flesh and the spirit, the kind that only occur in adolescence—an age when humans take their most radical plunges, because they enter on stage dressed only in a fragile armor of desires that are as voracious as they are naive. In this particular history, these adolescent passions were concentrated in even stronger doses, because they were contained within high walls which one could leave only on very special occasions; all reality was there. To these entirely physical and physiological elements should be added a frankly mystical fact: these were sixty boys locked in behind physical and spiritual walls, where they primarily lived for God.

It was said that the drama was composed of mysteries. What were the mysteries?

The mysteries were things beyond the imagination of the elect, things that exceeded their understanding. These things were sometimes terrifying, sometimes beautiful, but always inexplicable. They demanded faith, which must be blind. The word mystery, whenever invoked, cast a special light on things; it acted like a magic wand: one touch and everything became a mystery. At the time, mystery was everywhere in the Seminary: in the chapel (where God, who should be immeasurable, mysteriously inhabited a little box called the Tabernacle) and in the dormitory (where the mystery could be found underneath every bedsheet and each pajama, perhaps in the shape of sin), but also in the cafeteria, in the study room (for it was a mystery how one was able to study after lunch, or pay attention to the Rector's lectures) and in the classrooms (with undecipherable mysteries of mathematics and certain mysteries in the irregular conjugations of Latin verbs). Mystery was also in the orders that the Superiors gave and that could not be discussed, lest faith be compromised—and faith was full of mysterious truths, only known and revealed by God.

But who was God? How to understand, for example, that the same God could be represented by Superiors who were so different? How to love God above all else, without even knowing where God was?

All this, and much more, faith explained in such a manner that faith itself was pure mystery. But there were also mysteries in the hearts of the younger and older boys who tried to explain as best they could the new and complicated things they discovered. The most startling case of mystery was loving your neighbor above all else without falling in love with him, or being able to spend the whole day with him, frolicking during recess and studying in the study hall and even sleeping in the same bed, always besides him, precisely because he was loved all the time, and above all things, as Jesus had said—"Love one another, as I have loved you."

What kind of mysteries transpired between neighbors?

There were delightful, painful, and glorious mysteries. The delightful ones were when you could stay awhile with your beloved neighbor, without anyone noticing or criticizing the content of passion. It was also a delightful mystery to walk beside him on the soccer field after dinner, sensing the fragrance of his presence, and spying from the corner of your eye at his beautiful way of walking and praying the rosary; or to wait for the time to join him on the soccer field, during the recitation of the rosary. The painful mysteries were awful: when you missed him terribly and there was no comfort, even if you closed your eyes to imagine your beloved coming; or when it was not known for sure whether your love for your neighbor was reciprocated by the neighbor so immensely loved. But the most painful mystery of all was to love your neighbor with all your soul and so to commit sins against chastity, such as imagining your neighbor naked, or touching his hand covertly, or—already intoxicated with love—touching his cock during a film projection. Then, the mystery became extremely dangerous and could even lead to expulsion from the Seminary, of course in addition to committing one of the most mortal sins.

And the glorious mysteries?

Ah, those, unfortunately, seldom happened. This was when a boy loved his neighbor like himself, and his neighbor loved him like himself, and they could keep the secret between them in strict confidence, and love each other tirelessly, without fear. One then had the feeling of rising up to the Heavens, of being crowned above all the angels and the saints. In these moments, the mystery appeared to fade somewhat, and it became possible to understand why one suffered so much when loving according to Christ's commands.

Does that mean that the career path of the elect demanded a lot of effort?

Yes. The elect had to be prepared with iron and fire. For boys newly delivered from childhood, this was a time of trials, in which the supreme rule was to obey. To obey the Superiors, the regulations, the schedules. The authority of the Superiors was expressed, for example, in the right to read all the letters received by the seminarians and, if necessary, to censor them before they were delivered to their addressees; they also read all books received from outside, regulating the reading of the older and the younger ones; not infrequently, they forbade certain works that relatives themselves had sent to the children, because they were dangerous or too mundane. Even in the small library of the Seminary certain books were restricted by age (the Old Testament, for instance) and others were entirely forbidden and locked in a closet known as the Inferno, accessible only to the Superiors and the teachers. Some books that boasted their flaming spine in the Inferno: *Confiteor; Les misérables; Comment j'ai tué mon enfant; O outro caminho; Olhai os lírios do campo; Floradas na serra; L'homme, cet inconnu*. The Regulations expressly pointed to the nature and necessity of these prohibitions in order to preserve a pure mind for the future ministers of the Lord.

And the schedules, how were they obeyed?

There were three signals: the first two, with a ringing bell, served as warnings for the third, which was delivered with a sharp whistle, at the sound of which everyone rushed to form a line. Five minutes passed between one signal and the next. The Regulations prescribed punishment for those who arrived late in line.

How was the daily life of the elect in terms of their schedule?

More or less like this: they got up at 5:30 a.m. during the week (an hour later on Sundays). At 6:00 a.m., they all went to the chapel, where they said morning prayers, then engaged in collective meditation, followed by mass and a quick grace. At 7:30 a.m., breakfast in the cafeteria—coffee with milk, bread and butter. At 8:00 a.m. classes started, which lasted until 11:55 a.m., with a ten-minute break at 9:50 a.m. for a quick snack (bread and bananas). At noon they had lunch, followed by a brief visit to the *sanctum sanctorum* in the chapel. At 12:30 p.m., mandatory community work began: cleaning the house, the pigsty, and the chicken coop; planting, weeding, and harvesting in the garden, and sports equipment repairs. At 1:30 p.m., the first hour of study, which was mandatory. At 2:30 p.m., recess for a quick snack (bread or cake, also called *bolota*, in reference to the almost raw dough). At 3:00 p.m., alternatingly, one group went to the longer mandatory study hour, while the others went to play soccer; on Mondays, Wednesdays, and Fridays, the older ones played; on Tuesdays, Thursdays, and Saturdays, the younger ones. Only on Sundays there was soccer for both groups, albeit at different times. Those who did not like soccer could play tennis or volleyball—this was the preference of a group of sissy boys, and was hence considered a minor sport. At 5:30 p.m., they had dinner and collectively prayed the Angelus, right there in the cafeteria. At 6:00 p.m., mandatory recreation. Twice a week there were also mandatory games, for the older ones and the young ones respectively; then the famous Bottle Game took place—terror of the weak and oppressed. At 7:00 p.m., exhausted by the game, the students recited the rosary, alone or in groups. Only on Saturdays the rosary was strictly prayed in Latin, with the whole community walking in the courtyard in four parallel rows, back and forth, in a choreography that in this context might well be called sacred: *Pater Noster* forward, *Ave-Maria gratia* backward, then forward, then back and forth and back, until at the end of each set of ten Hail Marys they reached the next Our Father, starting off another dozen Hail Marys; by now the numbers, movements and voices made them drowsy, in a Latin evocative of distant, indistinct times of Christianity. At 7:30 p.m., they went up again for a mandatory study period. At 8:30 p.m., the community went to the chapel to say the evening prayer. Soon after, they had tea right there in the corridor, and then went to the lavatories, where they had ten minutes for their late-night ablutions. At 9:00 p.m., the lights went out and they slept. The older ones, however, still had an option to study until 10:00 p.m. in their pajamas.

What did the Regulations say about extra-curricular activities?

The Regulations provided for biweekly walks, with a stroll to the nearest beach. Once a month, there was a special trip to outlying farms, fields, and mountains, which were big events for the whole community. As for visits from parents and relatives, the Regulations determined that, apart from exceptional cases, these would be allowed exclusively on the second Sunday of each month. This was certainly one of the most unhappy things about the Regulations; very often, seminarians missed visitors who, unaware of the rules, arrived on the wrong Sunday. The only remedy was then to cry inside the bathroom, clinging to whatever parcel the family had left, unable to deliver it personally. The seminarians wept with longing but also with anger. God appeared an executioner at these times.

Did the Regulations govern everything?

Almost everything. According to the Regulations—a booklet given to each novice, on their first day at the Seminary—it was forbidden for older ones to talk to younger ones, except on some rare occasions: during the 12:30 p.m. community work, and at the end of the obligatory evening recess, when you could pray the rosary alone, in groups, or in pairs, always while walking on the soccer field. Besides having separate dormitories and study halls, the older ones and younger ones were assigned different spaces on the playground and in the cafeteria. Of course, it was forbidden for a younger one to enter the dormitory of the older ones, or vice versa. It was forbidden to talk in any of the house's rooms outside of recreational hours; mandatory silence ended only after one had reached the external patio and answered "Deo gratias" to the Prefect's "Deo gratias." It was forbidden to talk anywhere after the 7:00 p.m. recess. It was forbidden to go inside the dormitories, cafeteria, or study halls outside the prescribed schedule. It was forbidden to talk during meals, except on Sundays and holidays. At lunch and dinner there were regular readings of adventure books, or of the lives of saints; every day before finishing dinner, passages from the Roman Martyrology were read to identify the saints of the day and to declare their sufferings and virtues. It was strictly forbidden to converse in the chapel, in front of the Blessed Sacrament. It was forbidden to go through the gates of the Seminary and enter the "world." Besides holidays, one could only go out on special occasions: on community outings, during the processions of Rogation Days, for visits to the doctor, or to attend solemn masses in the city. It was even more forbidden to have private friendships and to touch hands in play during recess. If asked why, the Rector answered enigmatically: "Non clericat"—it is not suitable for clergy or seminarians for reasons of chastity, to which the instructor of ancient Greek would be quick to add: "Soma sema," meaning that the body is a tomb.

During this ascent to perfection, did they seek the death of all sins?

They sought the death of all sins. And their bodies become their graves.

In how many ways did one sin in those times?

In a variety of ways. In fact, in infinite ways. One committed the sins of laziness, envy, gluttony, concupiscence, salacity, pride, vanity, impurity, blasphemy, gossiping about others, sins of omission, of thought, word, and works, venial and mortal. Regulations and discipline were used as a weapon to combat sin and strengthen virtue. Hence it was mandatory to always wear a formal jacket, except at recess. Walking in line was also mandatory when going from one place to another: two straight lines, two meters apart, observing half a meter's distance between one student and another; the younger ones went ahead, the older ones followed behind. It was recommended to say the rosary while walking in line because it improved the report card's grade for behavior.

What did the sinners or truants have coming?

Punishment. According to the Catechism, Particular Judgement followed directly upon Death, while the Final Judgement would only come in the End of Times. According to the Judgment, there would be Heaven or Hell for all eternity. But at the Seminary, even before Death there existed many types of punishment, which may not have been eternal but were nonetheless troublesome. Getting out of line meant punishment. Kicking a pebble while walking in line meant punishment, as did whispering to one's front or back neighbor. You were punished with the Wall, with suspensions, with compulsory seclusion—incommunicado—and with expulsion in severe or recurrent cases.

Could one conceive this in terms of a biblical fall?

Yes, because being expelled meant a sort of original sin, feared like death or damnation. Those expelled from Paradise were isolated and kept incommunicado until their parents came to pick them up. They ate after the community had finished, sat apart in the chapel, and no longer participated in recess. They had earned the dishonorable epithet of "ex-seminarian." And they were thrown into the "World."

Were there many cases of expulsion?

Many. For the most diverse reasons. One of the older ones was expelled for drinking half a bottle of wine from mass, while entrusted with the duties of the sacristan. Another because he secretly smoked. Another because he was reading *Les Misérables*. Two were expelled for exchanging a kiss in the dressing room. Several for maintaining insistent private friendships. And there was the famous Inquisition of the Twelve, which lasted ten days and resulted in the expulsion of twelve boys—for their grave collective offense against holy chastity.

What other punishments were imposed before the Judgment of God?

Before God's Judgment, the punishment of the Wall was routinely administered: boys who talked outside the permitted hours, who left their line, who complained about food, or who came late had to lean against a wall during recess and were prohibited from socializing and talking to their peers. Standing straight up—looking at the world of normality from afar. The duration of the Wall depended on the nature of the transgression: one hour, two hours, or two two-hour breaks on successive days. In the case of a repeated offence, or if the punishment were not strictly observed (for example, if any talking occurred whilst they stood against the Wall), they could be separated for several days—which meant a very low participation grade and, hence, a red flag for expulsion. Another punishment was to "stay in seclusion," which differed from the Wall in that one had to stay in the chapel, praying and reading about the lives of saints, obviously in silence. The punishment of seclusion was applied on special occasions: on the day of a community outing, for example, or on the night of a film projection (which happened once a month). It is true that this punishment offered certain compensations, especially when many boys were punished and the Prefects of Discipline or Superiors were watching the film. The chapel then became a delightful playground, where the condemned talked, laughed, and perambulated leisurely, or even invaded the sacristy to eat a host, or went to the choir to play the organ. When there were mischievous students among those punished, they would hold veritable theatrical performances in the chapel, featuring imitations of funeral masses (dedicated to the soul of an especially disliked Prefect) and caricatural impersonations of the Superiors. Assuming God saw everything—both outside and inside the chapel—these boys did not hesitate to live it up in the place where He was most obviously present. They believed that they could disobey the Regulations at will, since penance neutralized the original sins committed during the penitential state. This proves that at least they understood the rudiments of Christian Doctrine.

What was the Participation Grade?

There was a participation grade (weekly) and grade for study (monthly). Once a week, the older ones and younger ones assembled in their respective study halls to learn their participation grades, which were read out loud by the Prefects. Examples of the more common infractions that lowered the score: tapping on a desk in the study hall, touching another boy, walking out of line, talking out of hours. Below a grade of eight, punishments were applied, usually half a day in strict silence in the study hall. Penalization increased as the grade decreased. Below three, the offender had to stand in silence against the Wall. Some students who had a large number of absences in addition to their low grade would be forbidden to talk for weeks. The punishment had to be carried out to the letter, or the time of their enforced silence would be doubled. This was the case of a boy named Foguinho, who ended up with his mouth shut for a month and a half. Just because he had the habit of talking to his neighbor in the adjacent bed. A grave sin.

And what did he talk about, between the sheets?

Nobody knew. In any case, Foguinho was one of the twelve sentenced and expelled during the so-called Inquisition.

What did the Prefects do?

They made sure that all regulations were strictly observed. They also determined and enforced minor penalties. In case of severe punishment, they sought the advice and approval of the Rector. There were four of them: two for the older ones and two for the younger ones. Every six months, the Rector appointed new incumbents for the position, chosen from those students whom he trusted. Even though they always belonged to the group of older students, the Prefects of the younger ones lived with the younger ones, slept in their dormitory and studied in their hall. Prefects were vested with the same authority as the Superior Fathers, since they served as their legitimate representatives. An example: to get out of the compulsory evening recreation, pupils needed the permission of one of the Prefects. Permission was required even to go to the chapel, to make spontaneous visits to the Blessed Sacrament (which, if done spontaneously, had a reputation for improving grades for behavior). This position of authority made the Prefects particularly feared. Even more so because they took advantage of this to protect their friends and "little fish" (their favorites)—because it was rare for a Prefect not to find at least one favorite, usually among the younger ones, among whom they moved freely. There were also those whom the Prefects pursued out of enmity, or natural antipathy. In any case, particularly younger novices and sissies routinely suffered at their hands, since it was very easy for the teenage prefects to behave like real authorities with the newcomers, who hardly knew the Regulations, or to those too delicate-looking boys.

What was a novice?

Novices were those who had just arrived from the outside world and didn't know anything about the local rules, and as a result incurred general contempt. Besides, the novice was usually a crybaby: he cried for anything and called his mommy. Or he wept in the bathroom, homesick. A newcomer remained in the novice category for a year and demanded a lot of holy patience from his "angel." An angel was a seminarian in charge of receiving a novice and teaching him everything: from how to kneel in the chapel and cut a banana for dessert to the fundamental points of the Regulations. Each novice had an angel and became his "pupil." There were good angels and bad angels. The good ones were friends with the pupils—but they were few. The bad ones took advantage, eating the sweets that the pupil received, threatening him with made-up reprisals, instilling fear of everything ("the food here has saltpeter, so whoever eats too much becomes a sissy") and poking fun at him for doing things wrong, calling him a "stupid tadpole" and spreading the news of his blunder. "Novice" was equivalent in meaning to "froglet," because he no longer lived in the water, but was not yet fully equipped for life on land. The froglets were witless. When they arrived in a group of people, the circle would break up in an instant: no one trusted a little boy who had barely emerged from his egg. The froglet would suffer without complaint, since the following year it would be his turn to scorn and mistreat the new froglets. Being a froglet was an initiation rite, in which one underwent a kind of internal circumcision—a specific, perennial mark that was imprinted in the center of the heart. It was the beginning of a brutal pain: leaving a mother's warm lap to fall into a world of strangers who lashed out like cannibals.

What else did the Prefect of Discipline do, besides controlling the community and bullying the tadpoles?

One of the Prefects used to dominate the position of assignment nominator, which significantly increased his prestige, because he could distribute community duties, as rewards or as punishments. The posts considered better included: being in charge of the storage room (where sporting materials were kept), acting as cafeteria servants (one ate well and a lot), and serving as librarian (who had access to the Inferno). The most loathed duties were: cleaning the lavatories and the house, being in charge of dirty clothes, serving as acolyte for masses, or as sacristan (chief and assistant). Except for the positions of janitor (responsible for a classroom) and nurse, which were in effect for one semester, all the others were renewed weekly, a fact that gave the Prefects considerable leverage in manipulating life in the community.

What other characters, whether secondary or not, took part in this drama of the lives and passions of the elect?

This drama included many characters of secondary importance. Sometimes they were backstage characters, like the washerwomen, who dropped by weekly to deliver their bundles of clean clothes and to pick up the dirty clothes of the priests and seminarians, without overstepping the limits of the visiting room. Also the nuns, who lived in the back of the Seminary and took care of the kitchen, were only seen behind the scenes. Teachers—priests and secular ones— entered the stage when they arrived every morning from the city to teach their classes, and were delivered and then returned by a Kombi van. The teachers were parish priests or assistants in parishes in the city and lived extremely busy lives. Perhaps this is why their classes did not excel in brilliance. In any case, the Seminary had few teachers and only four class groups, one for each grade of middle school. Aside from one or another's occasionally eager approach, the teachers ordinarily were not deeply involved in the lives of seminarians. As if by magic, they disappeared from the scene as soon as classes were over. There was also the old Father Confessor, who came every two weeks to listen to the seminarians' special sins and afterwards returned to his parish in the city to digest what he had heard.

Regarding the mention of terror caused by certain games: what was the Bottle Game about?

The Bottle Game was meant to heat up the spirit. Like a nighttime farewell to a busy day. And to tighten the muscles, encourage the spirit of emulation, and activate resilience. In the Bottle Game, anyone could discharge aggression accumulated during the day or the week. Those who could not, received the aggression of others and cried, because it was forbidden to complain—"a real man has to take it in silence." Others, to console themselves (because it lasted only half an hour), thought: a game is a game. But this game was also war. To form tough men, or as they said, men of fiber. There were those who in the Bottle Game suffered real Christian pains, taking beatings from Gethsemane to Calvary. The weaker ones were made to carry a cross. The pain and humiliation were too much to bear; so much that absent mothers were widely lamented, more or less like this: "Mother, mother, why did you abandon me?" Then they gazed at the sky, in search of help or relief from those who had plunged them into such misfortune. They might also scream for Jesus who had died for us, or beg for their tormentors to temper their wrath. Many thought they were suffering in the name of God. But God was not going to accept a sacrifice so stupid, so gratuitous as this. In short, the Bottle Game was as severe as the Last Judgment. Poor souls, who did not know how to escape from the demons! They would be taken not to the fires of hell, but through a corridor of smacking and whipping on all sides and on every inch of their flesh, until they got through the neck of the bottle.

How was this Calvary made tangible, how this Gethsemane revived?

Like this: twice a week, after dinner, an enormous circle was drawn on the floor of the soccer field, and the circle completed with a narrow bottleneck at the top. A catcher was chosen. With the catcher outside, the rest of players were inside the circle. After the countdown, the game began: everyone had to get out of the bottle and to avoid the catcher, who had singled out someone to seize. Since touching by hand was prohibited, each carried a handkerchief with a knot at the end. When he cornered someone, the catcher would hit the other boy with the handkerchief. That was the starting cry of a war of all against one. Everyone in one great mass then launched themselves onto the victim, hitting him with their handkerchiefs, and at that point the game became truly serious. The goal was to then try to prevent the victim from reentering the circle—only possible via the narrow bottleneck—dragging out the beating as long as possible. For the victim, pain and defeat were mixed in a multiplicity of ways. It was much worse when the catcher caught a victim far away from the bottle; then the beating began there and continued all the way back—a Via Crucis in a state of despair, evidenced by the contorted faces, discordant moans, and uncontrollable weeping of those who were beaten, suffered, and wet their pants in fear. The height of entertainment was trying to prevent the victim from getting into the bottle. At this point, the group would already be forming a corridor on the outside of the bottleneck. When he was finally able to get in, the victim was whipped with strokes of varying degrees of aggression. There would be screams in all tones, laughter, teasing, and cursing in disguise (cursing was a serious offense: certain cuss words could result in an expulsion). Since they could not say "faggot" or "son of a bitch," they rhythmically cheered in chorus: ma-ri-qui-nha, sis-sy-boy, sis-sy-boy. After that, the game resumed, with another catcher and renewed energies. Some particulars of the game: the catcher always selected an easy prey; the catcher never chased his friends or favorites; the catcher cultivated his craft with perfection, for instance by putting glue on the handkerchief's knot and waiting for it to dry; most participants followed suit, for everybody there would rather be a potential catcher than a victim; the victims were almost always the same and took a beating with dry glue, which was not unlike a hailstorm of rocks hitting the body. Someone could be very lucky and be saved in the middle of a beating by the ringing of the bell. Then the Bottle Game stopped immediately. The strongest boys laughed contentedly, relaxed, replenished, shaking off dust and sweat. The weakest ran to the sink. They hastily washed away any signs of the beating that could come off with soap and water. There were bruises that took weeks to disappear and that sometimes needed special care from the nurse. These were marks of defeat stamped on their backs, arms, or faces, revealing the humiliation of having been the weakest. These boys hurriedly cleansed themselves and shed their most uncontainable tears before quickly returning to the line in pursuit of perfection. Standing in line, quietly praying a chaplet of the rosary, they sometimes thought of the adulteress mentioned in the Gospel, who was stoned for her sins and finally saved by Jesus. Just maybe, next time Jesus would be merciful. In any case, the victims with expectant terror awaited the nights when a new Bottle Game would come. The most docile ones kept the game's marks for their Spiritual Bouquets, which afterwards they sent home on their mother's birthday (for example), with a card in which they wrote something along these lines: "To mommy dearest, this Spiritual Bouquet contains 30 short prayers, 10 chaplets, 35 Visits to the Blessed Sacrament, 30 masses and 150 sacrifices."

And Tiquinho, where was he?

Among the humiliated, whose nightmares he shared. Because of his fragility, during the Bottle Game he would experience an absolutely transformative event—as will be seen later.

What are the overall effects of these disciplinary games on the boys' virility, and in terms of their suffering?

Failure and frustration, ultimately. The weak stayed weak, and the sissies were confirmed as sissies, whereas the strong redoubled their strength.

It has been mentioned that the "world" presented many dangers. What happened during the vacation periods?

They tried to keep the Regulations in place, at least minimally. Before leaving for vacation (in July, or from January to February), the seminarians had to listen to a long lecture in which the old Rector explained in detail the ideal behavior of the elect during the holiday period: go to Mass every morning, pray chaplets of the rosary in church every night, always remain available to the vicar, no outings to the cinema, no reading books without the vicar's prior permission, obey your parents, set a good example for your siblings. And above all, avoid paths that lead to impurity. At this point, he always repeated the same words: "Remember that, according to the Gospels, the Virgin Mary entered Zacharias' home and greeted her cousin Isabel, but not her male cousin. It is better to be among equals. When visiting relatives, stay with male cousins and avoid female cousins to avoid temptations of the flesh."

Had the old Rector suffered a violent passion for a female cousin in his youth?

Maybe a passion so entirely shattering that it remained in his memory forever. In any case, when returning from vacation, the seminarians had to bring a certificate of good behavior, signed by the local parish vicar. It is true that the majority of the vicars had more important things to do than monitor seminarians on vacation. And they signed the certificates in the same way they held their masses and carried out baptisms: yawning. Evidently, the "dangerous world" was their natural habitat and presented nothing new—a repetition of small tasks, daily peccadilloes, and lots of beer in bars to quench the boredom. Upon returning to the Seminary, the young elect still found the evangelical truth well protected in all its purity behind those walls. The Superiors, the uncompromising old God, and the vicars were nothing but angels threatened by decay. Like Christ, the elect needed to prepare themselves to resist, before going out to preach the Word of God among the impious.

Is that why they retreated for three days in silence after their vacation?

Yes, in order to decontaminate the soul. So that the reign of discipline could be resumed with iron and fire, in search of Christian Perfection.

Of the Hungarian Rhapsody
and Correlated Passions

Why do you begin your recital of these memories with the Hungarian Rhapsody #2 by Franz Liszt?

Because its chords' winding lines seem to describe a most pathetic form of passion. But mainly because its sonorous contortions resonated with the boy Tiquinho as an expression of his personal sense of inadequacy.

Was Tiquinho versed in music?

No. He was just sensitive to it, like so many other boys in those days. The fact is that musical non-verbality allowed for rather subjective interpretations, making it a perfect conduit for translating the most inexpressible feelings that teemed inside. That is, if music opened their little boys' hearts, it was because they translated it in accordance with their inner experiences, and transcribed to their own liking the passions that the composers had poured into the score. This phenomenon frequently affected Tiquinho with the Hungarian Rhapsody #2.

When did this happen?

In the first days of the Seminary, when Tiquinho was still an inexperienced tadpole who always cried in a corner and wanted to return to his mother's arms. In those early days, there was music only rarely, on special occasions. Tiquinho had arrived only two weeks earlier and was still finding his way. He still knew little about the rules, especially since his angel was not very generous in giving explanations. Although excited, he did not know when he should start wearing the underwear his mother had made for his trousseau, as was requested by the priests. He looked into the matter. After explaining to him that he should have been wearing underwear since his arrival, the scandalized angel sent him off with a stern and definitive comment: "Walking without underwear is against the Regulations, because you are no longer a child." Tiquinho was delighted to know that he was no longer considered a child. So, he immediately headed for the closet, happily picked a pair of still-hard cotton briefs and, behind the closed door of a toilet stall, slowly put them on, eyeing himself in a portable compact mirror to see what a man without pants looked like. He left the stalls proud to finally have come of age. And so, pleased with his new life, he found himself in front of a room where some

boys sat listening to music. He waited outside, not knowing
whether he would be violating any part of the Regulations
if he entered. He then for the first time heard the heartrend-
ing chords of what he would later find out was Hungarian
Rhapsody # 2, a title he never forgot. Struck breathless by
the beauty of the music, he stood there in the shade, his eyes
and his ears popping with the intense clarity emerging from
those sounds. It was in this clarity that he noticed the presence of a boy sitting directly in front of him. How beautiful,
he thought. How beautiful, he repeated to himself. He is so
terribly handsome, he thought, without fully realizing that
this insistency sprang from his intoxicated flesh. His eyes
were enchanted, his head was spinning, and his ears were
sucking in the sounds, and everything merged in a whirlwind that sprang up like an immense pin that pierced some
point of his soul, thrusting into the flesh without origin or
direction. He blinked several times to escape, because he was
afraid. And he also blinked with anxiety, for he knew that
this beauty had imprisoned him, as had happened many
times before and would happen again many times afterwards. "Something must be wrong with me," he thought in
the midst of this marvel and fascination, because the boy
had already stridden into the air to the sound of painful
violins. He was afraid of the magma of contradictory emotions that engulfed him and that only ceased at great effort.
Walking alone during recess, he felt bitterness in admit-

ting that his coming of age was nothing short of a fiasco. Wearing underwear would not truly make him a man, not as long as he continued to feel "this way" for boys and men. Even more painful was the awareness that, part of him liked this feeling, while another part of him rejected the experience. From that moment on, the Hungarian Rhapsody never failed to provide him with an exact measure of his inadequacy. Listening to this music with inescapable melancholy and fascination, it was as if he heard his own heart beating. He tried in vain to decipher its pattern.

How did Tiquinho survive?

By making friends. Everybody in there tried to survive the same way. The community thus formed a mesh of so-called "cliques."

What was Tiquinho's clique like?

Comical, because it was based on a system of self-defense that included an absolute confidentiality among its members and its own vocabulary. "A piece" meant a handsome boy, "bomb time" meant a lecture by the Rector, "catilinarian" referred to Latin class, and "tractor" was a generic name for the older ones, whereas the Superiors were designated ambiguously as "superlatives," and the food (the main object of their sarcasm), why yes, was called "the lava"— because of the frequent heartburn following its ingestion—or sometimes "the washing"—a laconic but no less virulent allusion to this phenomenon—or even "the miracle of Lavoisier," in due remembrance of the law according to which nothing is lost in nature, and everything is transformed. The group consisted of five or six boys of the same cohort, who had sworn to trust each other blindly and who shared their most intimate problems and secrets, including their passions. To a greater or lesser degree, they were all called *mariquinhas*, sissies.

What were the characteristics of a sissy?

Fundamentally two: to not play soccer and to bathe daily. Since the older ones and the younger ones took turns playing soccer on designated days, they only bathed every other day. As a result, there existed a direct correlation between excessive bathing and a meager aptitude for soccer or, on the contrary, between the practice of soccer and an approach to bathing as only a necessity. Far-reaching conclusions were drawn from this: a sissy used talc, because a real man smelled of sweat. In fact, a man should "smell like cum"—and it was understood, by this hasty conclusion, that the accumulation of smegma under the foreskin indicated a generous amount of sperm and, therefore, of virility. There was a young man who became a record holder in virility, after spending two weeks without taking a shower. Naturally, he scratched himself more than a cowboy and proudly sported an erection that was as permanent as it was unrestrainable. Until the day that the old Rector publicly threatened him with expulsion—much to the delight of Tiquinho's group, who considered this a revenge that was also in a way a legitimization of their hygienic habits. Further sufficient—but not necessary—characteristics of the sissy included: playing volleyball, emitting cries of fear or surprise, being horrified by the Bottle Game, and gesturing in a somewhat swishy, fluttering manner. In fact, it was precisely because of the latter that Tiquinho's group came to be known as the "flock" (a name maliciously reinterpreted by the most daring as the "fairies"). Hence their nicknames, which were finally established as follows: in addition to Tico-Tico (Sparrow), they were Canary, Forpus (sometimes known, by the Flock's enemies, as Drag-ass—a dubious synonym for this particular species of South American parakeet), Seriema (a skinny boy from Mato Grosso) and Woodpecker (the intended meaning of which clearly varied according to the speaker's facial expression and tone of voice).

What had formed this clique and made it so tight?

The fact that they were hopelessly in love with other boys. Their favorite subjects and biggest secrets revolved around these passions, which were sometimes fleeting, sometimes devastating. Theirs was undoubtedly a group of small aesthetes, judging by the refinement of their tastes in terms of clothing, male beauty, popular or classical music, and even in the care with which they prayed and asked for forgiveness for their sins. Once could say that they lived crucified between the call of God and the beauty of men. Notable, for example, was the liveliness with which the Flock promoted contests to elect the most beautiful boy of the older ones, younger ones or newcomers—voting, disputing and sometimes even launching a fan club for their "favorite," as they called the object of their love. But God's call also strongly manifested in their spiritual life, which was replete with ascetic claims, dramas of moral conscience, and fears of sin. There were those who claimed to be missionaries, set to convert the Indians and pagans. This was the case with Seriema and Forpus. During the period of the year that was devoted to Missionary Work, they ecstatically participated in special activities. They wrote and presented religious dramas with allusive titles ("Passion and Death of St. Francis Xavier in the East," in which they improvised oriental music with a handsaw, and managed with the help of makeup and old colored curtains to make the actors look perfectly like Japanese characters), they made new chaplets whose proceedings were destined for the Missions, and they took the lead in organizing Communal Spiritual Bouquets destined for the Missions in Africa and Asia, proffering the greatest sacrifices for China, where many martyrs were said to have died in the name of the Christian faith at the hands of the Communists—which was beautiful and moving. Most of the clique was obsessed with the virtue of purity, for which they lived in penance, because they were especially prone to the corresponding sin. They prayed on their knees on top of corn kernels, or put stones under their pillows and even put a self-made sackcloth around the waist, depending on the severity of the temptations and scruples. They also devoured biographies of the Saints of Purity, whose birthdays were celebrated with special mortifications. On August 15 (Saint Stanislau Kostka, representing "angelic innocence"), on June 21 (Saint Aloysius Gonzaga, patron of chaste youth), and on May 6 (Saint Dominic Savio, the first fifteen-year-old saint) they promised "not to approach anybody whilst praying the rosary," or "to avoid looking at anybody's legs during the soccer game"—by penalty of mortification. And they prayed, together or separately: "Angelical Dominic Savio, help us imitate you in your love of Jesus and make sure that, while committing, like you, to choose death before sin, we reach eternal salvation." But after these moments of great spiritual elevation, the Flock in one voice and amid lamenting sighs recognized that after all "the flesh is weak." Resigned to this fact, they continued to suffer, sometimes delighting in the sin of being in love—in thoughts, words and, sometimes, through what they called "works."

How could one be in love through "works"?

The story of Canary, Tiquinho's best friend, illustrates this well. He was a skinny boy who, because he was always jittering and talking like a chirping canary, had been thus rebaptized. Canary loved a soccer player of the older ones, whose nickname, Log-Log, referred to the unusual thickness of his member. Canary felt an irresistible attraction towards him that, to his disgrace, flowered right there in the rosebud of his ass. Almost in tears, Canary came to tell Tiquinho how he had just finished sinning "in works"—and this, in his own personal parlance, meant that Canary had masturbated with his finger stuck in his ass thinking of his favorite. He afterwards felt terribly guilty and was fearful of eternal condemnation, so that Tiquinho systematically referred him to the confessor, who finally managed to soothe Canary. But not long thereafter, the confession exonerated him to resume the same works. From then on, Canary made empty vows and suffered when he broke them. Only on soccer days did he overcome his scruples. He climbed one of the eucalyptus trees surrounding the field and from the top chirped Log-Log's name in all tones, every time his favorite took possession of the ball. Underneath, the Flock was amused, affectionately mocking their friend who "rooted for a team of one." During these recesses, the beauty of man was victorious over the perennial distinction between earth and heaven.

Which were the pleasures of heaven?

In heaven, one can imagine, they enjoyed seeing their favorites, and possessing all delights with no limits. This included masturbation, private (so-called) friendships, and other less common forms that were within reach of hand, eye, and thought. The whole community, and not only the sissies, was teeming with pleasure. In those days, sex was the most common, delectable, and gossiped about subject.

What were the less obvious forms of celestial pleasure?

For example: the boys disputed who was responsible for cleaning the pigpen and the chicken coop, considered among the least desirable chores in the house. Yet as a matter of fact, cleaning was also as an excuse to watch pigs, roosters, and ducks mate—often at the instigation of the cleaners. But since they worked little and instead enjoyed themselves, the place of course stayed dirty, to the point that religious services in the chapel nearby were affected by the smell. Another example of less obvious pleasures: there was a boy known to get aroused whenever he saw flies mating; in the summer, the proliferation of flies made him particularly horny. He kept asking for permission to go to the bathroom, feigning haven fallen victim to spells of diarrhea.

Was there a lot of courtship in those days?

In those days, boys courted each other in all corners and settings. Sitting in the study hall, in the chapel, in the cafeteria, in the classroom. Lying in the dorm, where court-ships fructified in dangerous waters. Afoot while walking in line, while praying the nocturnal chaplet, while playing soc-cer or watching the players, or even during the punishment against the Wall, flirting from a distance but with focused intensity. In fact, the boys' insistence was as admirable as their imagination. Since private friendships were strictly prohibited, they invented brilliant ways of overcoming these limitations. For example, they saw each other in the storage room, where sportsmen got together to mend balls and arrange repairs. Since the storage room was in the base-ment, it was possible to get close to your favorite between mending one patch and another and, with some luck, to exchange slight touches of indescribable flavor. During less frequented times of the day, it was also possible to provoke some hand-play; and then you could even get to furtive touching that almost came to physical violence, when shorts were lowered amid cheeky jokes. The storage room was the scene of improvised contests for the hairiest chests, juiciest thighs and—supreme delight—bulgiest members; on such occasions, the dénouement would take a less subtle form, such as that of one or more uncontrollable, unforgettable ejaculations. The courtships also flourished during study hours from nine to ten at night, which was allowed only for the older ones. Without the presence of the Prefects—who were usually too tired to study at this hour—students striv-ing to appear assiduous took advantage and changed their desks in order to form pairs in the hall. Sometimes couples "went to the bathroom" for purely coincidental physiological needs. The clearest proof that they in fact did not study sufficiently was the large number of pajamas that stood up like tents in the desert, or that were clearly stained by the forceful passage of love. While less quiet, the mandatory working hours after lunch provided further opportunity for complicated amorous encounters, because they allowed for contact between older ones and younger ones. It was common for couples consisting of boys disparate in size and age. The same disparities occurred when the seminarians prayed the rosary, strolling on the soccer field at the end of the evening's mandatory recreation session. There, the sweethearts (who did not dare to call themselves that!) also took advantage of the temporary permission for the older ones to join the younger ones, and they went to pray the rosary not in groups but in pairs. The invitation usually came from an older one who approached a younger one and, in a veiled (or, perhaps, timid) manner, said something along the lines of: "Let's walk?"—which meant a little bit of everything: courting, being close, missing each other, loving each other, looking at each other, enjoying. Then the soccer field filled with couples praying the rosary with special devotion, overwhelmed with emotion. It was at once saintlier and more delectable; each word of the Salve-Regina, Ave-Maria and Padre Nostrum could become a come-on and a declaration of love, when seasoned with enigmatic smiles and convivially scintillating eyes. Divinity itself was called upon to share this pleasure which, oh so fleetingly, was greedily imbibed and would later provoke longing sighs. As if proving God's consent.

Couldn't one speak of enchantment mixed with sacredness?

This mixture existed and was limited to that one space—the soccer field—which, in a way, benefited from it. Even though not all of them were couples, it was on the soccer field that the cliques got together during evening prayer or mandatory recess. The seminarians prayed, ambled, laughed, gossiped, and obligingly expounded their most intimate feelings to each other. All this on the soccer field, which was like a great mother who welcomed everyone without discrimination or censorship. One might say that the tenderness exchanged between the children spilled over into the space of the field. Consequently, they loved it, because it was a communal space of love. Tiquinho would live this feeling in a not very conscious but very intense way, as we shall see.

Why was it said that dating in the dormitory led into dangerous waters?

Because there the level of vigilance was heightened twofold. After the seminarians went to bed, one of the Prefects used to circulate for a long time through the dormitory's central corridor, until he was sure that everyone had fallen asleep. Hence, meetings could only take place afterwards and with great caution, so as to not wake up any of the invigilators. On the other hand, courtship in the dormitory allowed more comfort and, once the initial obstacle was overcome, unparalleled tranquility.

Did they love each other in the dorms?

Let's assume so, because there it was possible to get closer to a sense of mystery by raising another's bed sheets. The dorms were the scene of both serious love affairs and mockeries. Serious relationships meant sleeping together for hours and breaking the barrier between attached bodies. The mockeries were of course painful for some boys, while others enjoyed themselves at their expense. Sad, for instance, was the love affair of Forpus, one of the Flock's members. Forpus was in love with a classmate who slept in the other corner of the dorm. He used to get up at dawn, cross the room, and kneel down next to the bed of his favorite, trying to romantically contemplate him under the pale red light that stayed on at night. Once, at the apex of such contemplation, he was amazed to hear his favorite ask him in a strange but clear voice: "Do you like me?" After the first shock, which brought his heart to his mouth, Forpus replied almost sobbing with emotion: "I do." And the favorite: "Do you really like me, as a woman?" Forpus hesitated at first, but his bouncing heart pushed the words out of his mouth: "I love you for all eternity, just like a woman." And the other: "In that case, would you let me put it in your ass?" Forpus, with an even more agitated heart, quickly replied to avoid any sign of rational hesitation: "I would let it slip in all the way, for all eternity."

The favorite then burst out in unromantic laughter, followed by more laughter that came like an echo from the nearest beds. Only then did Forpus realize that he had declared himself to the wrong boy, although the bed was in the right place. He started to cry, realizing that he had fallen into a jointly plotted trap. And he crossed the dormitory in a dishonorable return, casting shattered sobs as he passed. To the Flock's woe, he was expelled shortly afterwards. This occurred in Tiquinho's second year.

Was there no similarity between the soccer field and the infirmary as spaces of love?

If memory serves, there was. To the infirmary came not only physically ill boys, but also many who, victimized by passion, came down with inexplicable and very high fevers, to the point of having ulcerating lips. In fact, the infirmary became a kind of refuge for those suffering in love. And this was thanks to a young man named Big Sweet Marcos who, being so competent and committed, held the position of nurse for an unprecedented term of almost two years without interruption. Despite being much older than the others, Marcos suffered from a shyness as outsized as his build. He lost his voice when talking to the Superiors and blushed when confronted with the semi-nakedness of the pupils to whom he administered injections. But he was particularly tender towards those boys who, assailed by strange fevers, came to recover under his care. Only then he opened up to the point of transfiguration. During his constant visits to the sick, he, who could barely utter a "good morning," tried to amuse them with jokes and anecdotes. Especially at night, before retiring to bed, he liked to tell them long stories in which men flew like angels and became wonderful heroes. Laughing in an unrestrained manner, he called the boys by tender and unusual pet names: "my little bug," "cute little cabbage," "sweet pie," "little blue Lulu," "green Lulu," "silver Lulu," "dulce de leche," "my pumpkin," and other extravagances bestowed under the spell of love. In those moments, the boys thought he was a bit crazy, but still they absorbed his affection, which undoubtedly helped to cure their wounds, of equivocal diagnosis.

Was Big Sweet Marcos in love with the sick?

Not just with the sick and not just in love. One night, a Prefect found Marcos sniffing ether, inside a stall that had inadvertently been left open. Then everything became clear. The fluctuation of his temper was in direct proportion to the ether that he sniffed in abundance, every night—and it is possible that he did it precisely to be able to love without hindrance. Everyone regretted his expulsion. Even with the changes that would occur later, the infirmary was never again a nest where the wounds of passion healed. Other spaces would appear. But nothing so radically romantic.

The boys were said to use their hands, eyes, and thoughts for enjoyment. And their cocks? How was their relationship with their cocks?

Crucial and anxious. Since cocks were rarely able to show themselves in the open, a cock on display in a rigid state was as delicious as a holiday and provoked true stupefaction. The boys, especially the most sensitive ones, for months remembered the fallible image of a hard cock. Tiquinho felt a mixture of terror and ecstasy in front of another boy's member, but he did not let terror repress his longing to touch the object of his dreams. However, there were cases in which, due to Christian scruples, repulsion imposed on attraction, and love wore a mask of terror. This was the case of a boy whose fear of cock was such that one could speak of phallic paranoia. One night, he got up screaming and took off across the dormitory like a rocket to the room of the Spiritual Director. They say he apparently had seen the devil. But no. He had just noticed, in a not-so-accidental glance, his neighbor's hard cock in bed. The attraction generated an opposite movement, but was not diluted. On the contrary, it fed on desire and grew until it became untenable.

And masturbation: was it a common practice to seek pleasure in solitude?

One could speak of a real epidemic, actually. Masturbating was known not only as "jerking off," but also as "killing alligators" and "spanking the monkey." At that time, fears of eternal hell fire matched the impetuosity with which magma poured from their little bodies, which longed for both holiness and pleasure. On confession days, long lines would form in front of the confessional, from which, at end of his shift, the old Confessor would yawn out of boredom from such a repetition of this solitary sin. But truth be told, they never admitted to jerking off in honor, or in remembrance, of their "neighbor," assuming that the confessors would feel more benevolent about impure loneliness than about vices committed by two or more boys, as we will soon see. The sin of touching oneself was so rampant that at times one exciting story was enough to spread within a circle of friends, and for the entire group to suddenly disperse as if charmed by a spell, each offering a different pretext. But after changing course countless times, each invariably turned in the direction of the lavatories, where they locked themselves in the stalls and clambered on the steep slopes of pleasure within hand's reach. Memory has kept almost intact the barely repressed moans that filled the lavatory, in the shower stalls—the most suitable for those moments of inner happiness that tore openings towards the world. The scene would be like this, if shot from a camera crane on tracks where the cart of the imagination would glide along placidly: bathroom doors closed for extensive periods of time, showers sometimes torrential and then halted. The crane rises without haste, until revealing over the walls the first stall on the left: Lourival masturbating almost without taking his dick out of his pants, with a technique meant to make his sin less obvious. Second stall on the right: Toninho masturbating, working his left hand with extreme agility. Third stall to the right: Mané lasciviously licking his lips, touching his enormous flagpole with squinting eyes of pleasure. Fourth stall on the right: what a surprise! Two boys in the fourth stall (which was the darkest and safest), two boys, wide-eyed at the simple mutual touch of their hard sticks, exceedingly close to levitating into the air by the touch of their most sacred points. From the fifth to the sixth stall, a teenager almost perched on top of the dividing wall, seeking inspiration from his neighbor's masturbation. It is hard to believe that he could even balance himself there, simultaneously clinging to the wall with his left hand, and to his own member with his right hand. There are still the stalls on the left, but there is no need to continue the description, which would run the risk of becoming redundant. Also because the celebration continued with squealing in the dormitory, with muffled squealing to avoid groaning, collective squealing from rows of beds that slightly trembled like an earthquake that sprung not from the earth, but from their abdomens.

Was sex ubiquitous in those days?

In addition to being omnipresent, sex was polyvalent, even against the inflexible will and often manifest wrath of God. The sermons insisted on this point, as did the frequent lectures by the Rector and the Spiritual Father. Purity was the virtue that fertilized the field of all other virtues. "Do not touch your own body too much," they urged—so as not to awaken the demon's fury. Nor, much less, to become too attached to each other, because the love of God was the opposite of the selfishness of friendships that, because they were exclusive, ended by creating opportunities for sin. "If one is not good, two should be avoided. Three is always best," said the old Rector, with his finger raised and his trembling lips moving more dramatically than the words required. According to him, vigilance should be instilled continuously along with the mortification of all the senses.

What mortifications formed their Christian conscience?

Many, besides punishments. On a movie night, for example, eyes were often collectively mortified. As soon as a kiss started on the screen, the projectionist was ordered to cover the lens with his hand. There were timid whistles of revolt. But the shouting became downright festive when the hand, tired or impatient, was withdrawn at the height of the libidinous act, which had lasted much longer than the Christian imagination could assume of a cinematographic kiss.

Was divine wrath frequently made manifest?

Yes. In truly biblical or even medieval outbursts. A famous and unforgettable event, stinging like red-hot iron in guilty and innocent consciences alike, was known as the "Inquisition of the Twelve," which took place in Tiquinho's second year. It all happened right after the start of the holidays in July. Groups had been appointed to clean the building before classes resumed. A Prefect of the older ones, by the name of Andreolli, organized a team composed of his friends to clean the lavatories. He included a boy from the younger ones named Matias, whose fame as a fairy was such that even the saintliest students knew some of its scandalous details. It was never completely clear which sins lead up to this Day of Judgment. What is certain is only that suddenly all communal activities were suspended indefinitely and that the Seminary was plunged into a climate similar to the dark calm preceding a storm. Initially, there was a laconic rumor that the six members of the team cleaning the lavatories were caught *in flagrante* in actions violating chastity. The rumor spread like the plague. The group had done a swap-and-change. No, the group had used Matias for lustful actions. Or, no: there had been very serious hanky-panky. Serious how? Four boys grabbed Matias and lowered his shorts, while Andreolli himself (or was it Andreozzi?) humped him. No: Andreozzi took him into a stall and closed the door, while the other four whooped and splashed each other with water. Then the Rector arrived just in time to see that obviously everyone had a hard-on under their shorts. Did anything else happen? Nobody was sure during those ten days in which the life in the community revolved exclusively around the rigorous investigations carried out by the priests. An atmosphere of heavy spiritual retreat, with continuous prayers and meditations, was imposed. At the end of each afternoon, the Rector reported on the results obtained from the latest confessions, in words both indirect and foreboding. Gradually, new characters were involved in the scandal, which rippled outward from the lavatory and spread to other sectors with a foul smell that spared no one. And that caused a general panic; with the exception of a few irreproachable saintly persons, all seminarians ended up feeling potentially involved, deep down in their anguished consciences. Cold sweats rolled down everyone's back each time an interviewee returned to the study hall or the chapel, sometimes with red eyes, sometimes with the pallor of a corpse. It seems that Matias had become the pivot at the heart of everything. Stories were pulled from his persona as if he were a spool of thread. It was said that Matias had also been repeatedly attacked in the storage room and in the locker room throughout the previous semester. In the storage room, the older boys lined up to enter Matias. In the locker room, something similar happened, but in a different scenario: a kind of corridor was formed entirely with priests' hanging cassocks, which seminarians used on festive days and for solemn masses. There, behind the darkness of the robes, the boys reveled in little Matias' lavish nakedness. Coerced by violent exhortations and threats of eternal condemnation, students often ended up accusing each other and fearing one another. During this period, it was not uncommon to experience sudden outbursts of crying in the study, during recess, in the chapel, and even in the cafeteria where *The Pearl of Virtues*—a little book that exalted the importance of chastity—was read aloud in alternation with the Apocalypse of Saint John. The Flock kept silent and felt intimidated, as if living through the Last Judgment. None of them dared to exchange words with each other during these ten days that shook up the life of the Seminary. Following the latest investigations, twelve suspicious students were singled out and detained incommunicado, a sign of imminent expulsion. On August 9, the day of Saint John Vianney, Holy Curé of Ars, things unfolded as if at the

end of a great parturition of pus and rot. In a solemn session
in the chapel, the Rector and the Spiritual Director assembled the whole community to report that, with the grace of
God, the work of purging had been completed. With a loud
voice and in an imposing tone, the names of the twelve culprits were announced. Although all the students, for better or worse, knew about the events, they made no reference to concrete facts. The Rector mentioned only serious
acts of licentiousness, unacceptable in elected youths, and
thanked the intervention of the Holy Curé of Ars, Patron of
Priestly Vocations, who had enlightened them in the search
for, and elimination of, the source of impurities. The community was urged to follow his example in the cultivation
of chastity, mother of all virtues and of discipline. The Rector ended the sermon with a "Sursum corda," and then offi-
ciated the Blessing of the Holy Sacrament. The following
day, the Twelve had already disappeared into the whirlwind
of the world, while the remaining elect raised their hearts
to heaven. They carried a new scar and a little more fear.
Nobody ever forgot the Inquisition of the Twelve. From
then on, even the Flock lost much of its luster. It was never
the same again, even though the friendships in its inner circle continued and self-defense strategies were reinforced.
But its joy waned. Love for men had become substantially
more inaccessible. God had won in an unequal fight. And

who would dare to protest? Perhaps, in the depths of their hearts, they were awaiting an opportunity for retribution.

An impossible retribution is what they were waiting for.

Of the Beauty of God

As time went by, were there no changes in the style of education that, with iron and fire, informed the spirit of the chosen?

Yes, thanks to the new "aggiornamento" guidelines of the Second Vatican Council. What is certain is that at the beginning of Tiquinho's third year the old style was transformed, with the replacement of the old superiors by young priests. Especially the delicate Spiritual Director, who had been scandalized, protested before the bishop and worked to suppress the Seminary's too rigorous climate. So the Regulations were relaxed, although they continued to be the Regulations, because the changes were not that radical, as we will see. In any case, the students felt an undeniable relief. There were no more lines, the punishments became less rigid, the separation between the older and younger ones was no longer as strict, nor was it mandatory to wear the formal jacket. The new, less traditional pedagogical orientation ended up valuing the subjectivity of each seminarian in (relative) interaction with the subjectivity of the young Superiors. By undoing certain barriers, the community entered a whirlwind of revelations, and in just a few months the Seminary evolved into a realm of concentrated passions—Christian passions which of course behind these walls were always crushed within mute hearts, trying in vain to break boundaries. Under the new Superiors, this uncompromising God who reigned, ordered, and punished now also scandalously loved. Overflowing like a God who had just fallen in love.

Who was this God that was so passionate?

God was two and not three, as is generally believed. But this did not mean that he was a two-headed being, as one might hastily infer. Rather, in this case there were two perfectly distinct and even contradictory entities that shared a single divinity. Here, the drama was coordinated by the two new Superiors who had arrived to fill the positions of Rector and Spiritual Director. The former dressed in a rigorously black cassock. The latter preferred lighter outfits and all year long wore impeccably white robes—"transparencies to not cover the soul," he sometimes said. In short, these were two beautiful beings—not only in spirit—who reigned with an air of eternity, and who created love everywhere around them.

Why was God breathtaking?

God was breathtaking because both priests were resplendent, fascinating and different, in the full strength of their youth. The Spiritual Director, who oversaw the inner lives of the boys, had smooth blond hair and transpired maternal tenderness. The new Rector, in charge to enforce solid discipline, was of Portuguese descent and flaunted the sensual dark skin of the Iberians. His gait called to mind both the poise and irreproachable bearing of a purebred colt.

How come they reigned with an air of eternity?

They seemed spiritually omnipotent in that universe inhabited by sixty desirous children, among whom they began to share out their divinity or, rather, to compete in offering their magnanimous divinity, which, in addition to punishing and guiding according to sacred Christian principles, also loved scandalously, as I mentioned before. In other words, their severity was a pretext for the floodgates of love to open.

Why is it said that they created love all around them?

Simply because love flowed out of their beauty. That is, their love was put forth as entirely sufficient. The nascent (but no less overwhelming) desires of the sixty elects came to behold two supreme images that they began loving with the fierceness of those seeking an absolute love that was absolutely theirs. With those two priests arriving on the scene as a volcanic crater that suddenly erupts, the Lord's little chosen ones plunged into a kind of libidinal lava and began to vie for them with all their weapons and rights. There were demonic streaks in this generally subterranean contest, although these occasionally sharpened into extremes of cruelty, as will be mentioned. The truth is that because of the extreme heat of love the boys entered a cycle of chronic jealousy.

How might one describe this fascination with two entities similar in function, yet so distinct in personality?

It could be called the Mystery of the Passionate Authority. The two Superiors were loved as visible (almost palpable) representations of God.

And how could one worship divinity, something so transcendent, through loves affairs so carnal?

This was only possible because divinity had become incarnate, and transcendence occurred in the quotidian reality of their lives.

Then God definitely had a body like humans?

Definitely. God was present not only in the message of those two priests. God had a body. And it was for the flesh of this God—divided into two—that the seminarians yearned like worshipers of absolute love. Absolute in the sense that they were seeking its ultimate consequences.

Was this love conscious?

Not entirely. But it undoubtedly was less conscious in the younger ones than in the older ones. When the Rector and the Spiritual Director arrived during recess, right after lunch, they flocked in their direction. The boys interrupted their activities to receive their blessing. It was from that moment on that each day the two made their triumphal entry into the concrete world of their little worshipers. Before then, they had remained abstract and distant entities, who maintained order in the house and taught some classes in the morning.

What was the saintly name of this duo?

The dark-haired one (let's say the dark representation of the Lord) was called Father Augusto, or Father Rector. The blond one (a most delicate image of the divinity) worked as the Spiritual Director and he was called Mário, but he preferred being called Father Marinho—"marine blue," he liked to joke, in reference to the color of his eyes. They said that he had studied with the Carmelites, hence his strong taste for mystical life.

You mentioned libidinal lava and demonic streaks in relation to the enormous love that the boys in no time devoted to them. How did this love come about in practice?

The love that poured from the two young priests took root in varying degrees and bloomed in all directions, despite the fact that the so-called "private friendships" continued to be expressly prohibited and extreme care was taken in addressing "affective problems" among the seminarians. Against these prescriptions, the environment— if this were possible to examine with a magnifying glass —looked like a great feast of passions. Passions that started evidently in God; thence, the only legitimate love (because it was sacred) was between the boys and their superiors—a reflection of the bond between creature and creator. Father Augusto, for example, liked to pick favorites who in addition to "little fish" were also called "sellotape" in the local jargon. Every month, or week, or fortnight, the little fish changed—invariably a teenager from the oldest group. Then there were silent competitions between the dethroned and the new occupant of the throne. Once, a former sellotape took advantage of his position as a cafeteria attendant and surreptitiously poured at least half a glass of hot pepper sauce into the sweet pumpkin jelly of his rival, the Rector's new protégé. A lot of crying ensued on both sides, especially since chili pepper in the mouth burns more when acts of passion are involved. The aggressor, threatened with expulsion, shortly afterwards spontaneously decided to leave the Seminary, bitter for having lost the loving favor of God. On another occasion, such jealousy exploded in a no less a cruel way: one of the Dean's little fish (a particularly unfriendly exemplar) was wearing pajamas to the toilet shortly before bedtime, when something fell on his head; touching the object, the boy felt the sticky surface of the one animal he considered the most disgusting of all: a toad—a small one, but nonetheless a toad. He instantly started screaming and ran across the dormitory as if taking part in an impromptu nightly marathon, taking refuge in his protector's room. From then on, he was allusively called Toady—with a double pejorative meaning. For that matter, when his period of reign went on for too long, Toady (who was a blond and porcelain-like ephebe) was the victim of another famous incursion: in his wardrobe (each student had his own), he once found a very milky chocolate bar filled with raisins—an indisputable sign of affection from his Rector; or at least, that's what he imagined, judging by the ostentatious manner in which he began to gobble down the chocolate bar for breakfast the next morning, well in sight of everyone. Only after the second generous bite did Toady realize that he was eating pellets of goat poop covered with toothpaste—apparently seasoned with lots of sugar and cinnamon. There were other anonymous and almost daily attacks. I can recall a particularly imaginative one. Because Toady tended to be a hypochondriac, he once wanted to take a urine test on account of pains in his kidneys. How terrified he was when on collecting the first urine of the day he saw it boil till the point of overflowing the flask. Horrified as if he had leprosy, he ran to the infirmary unable to speak a word, wearing on his face a dead man's pallor. It took the nurse no time to discover that someone had put acid salts in the bottom of the container. None of these cases caused official reprisals, since the aggressor remained anonymous. But countless were the outbursts of laughter throughout the entire community. Since in that closed environment passions bloomed intensely, the older ones held outright competitions in which nothing was off limits among themselves. To be in the Rector's favor, the adolescent boys went as far as snitching on each other. This was the case of the young lad called Pouting-Lips (he, for whatever reason, cried a lot), who made lists of all transgressions committed by his peers, so that he could hand them over to the Rector. This created an epidemic of vigilantism in which they themselves started controlling the discipline, since each was spying on the other—excepting only one's groups of friends. Hence, this was also a beneficial period for the "cliques," since it was necessary to protect oneself. Father Augusto evidently noticed the danger of this situation and interrupted the cycle of baiting by delivering a two-hour lecture against betrayal; he recalled Judas, a wretch who never managed to understand how much the Lord loved

him: and he ended by emphatically mentioning the infinity
of God's love, which knew neither limits nor privileged ones.
Of course, the boys were unable to take his words completely seriously. Even if some were propitiously loved for
their beauty, sweetness, and allure, others were particularly
disliked for opposite reasons. A classic example was the case
of Bento, a boy from the Amazon region who also responded
to the nickname Jaguar-Bubble-Gum. A superficial examination of Bento's appearance makes the reasons for this sur-
name crystal clear: pockmarked face, grinning teeth, hooked
nose, bent body, stumbling gait. To this condition was added
the fact that nature had not endowed him with great intelligence, whether for Latin, mathematics, history, or geogra-
phy, this despite his natural inclination towards literature
(which he often confused with cheap oratory). He further
had the unpleasant tic of bobbing his head compulsively,
as if to frighten off invisible flies. Perhaps because of scruples of a moral kind, he had become obsessed with personal
cleanliness: he kept washing his hands, especially after he
touched something; to not make them dirty, he picked up
the objects with his fingertips only; before lunch and dinner, he washed them for a long time and put them in the
pockets of his pants, until it was time to eat. For these reasons, he was a preferred victim of the wrath of the Rector,
to whom he devoted an immeasurable love, which was still
not sufficient to help him better learn the Latin declinations

in the classes that Padre Augusto taught in the third and fourth years. Hence, Bento Jaguar-Bubble-Gum often took a beating during these classes; he received blows of rulers on his back and erasers on his head, and sometimes he left school with his face all streaked with colored chalk: each trace corresponding to the teacher's irate reaction against the shocking innovations that Bubble Gum introduced to the language of Virgil and Ovid. Not that he didn't try. Trying to compensate for his faults with piety, he spent part of his free time in the chapel, praying with his showy wide ribbon of the Sodality of Our Lady. And he longed so much for love that, reading a chapter by a French mystical author, he decided to change his life radically. Because he was actually more inclined to reading book jackets—he said he had difficulty concentrating—he unfortunately did not get to the next chapter, which examined the failures of understanding that the mystic encountered ahead and that he, Jaguar-Bubble-Gum, would experience in his own skin after having candidly opted for a rather peculiar form of holiness: smiling.

And how can one be holy only with smiles?

First of all, by strictly following the prescriptions of the French mystic, for whom the smile had the strength of appeasement, sweetness, calmness, irradiance. Encouraged by the Spiritual Director, Bubble Gum at a theatrical performance in public read an excerpt of the mystic's writing, which said things like this: "When Christ's tree makes us tired and hurting, it is necessary to have the strength to smile benevolently. Because the smile is a form of benevolence that reflects inner joy. Brothers, let us be carriers of smiles and, doing so, sow joy." Bubble Gum took everything so seriously that, in conversation with his clique, he started devising an Order of the Smile, whose members called themselves the Enlightened Little Brothers and would spread throughout Brazil, converting Brazilians to the smile and thus making the whole country happier: from the Indians of the Amazon to the university "pofessors," as he said. Bubble Gum spent at least a month in the greatest excitement and even promised to write the Book of Rules of the new Order, as well as a popular booklet prophetically called "Instead, pain prevails in the air," in which he intended to explain how to replace pain with joy.

And why did such effort in smiling generate so many misfortunes?

After that month of enlightenment, during which Bubble Gum maintained a tireless smile even during meals, the Rector accidentally took charge of destroying the Order, its Book of Rules, and the popular booklet. During a Latin class, Bubble Gum committed, smiling all the while, a particularly horrendous crime against the lingua mater—at least, so it is told, because of the unusually violent reaction of the Rector, who hurled books, pens, erasers, chalk, and everything he found within hand's reach. Then he scratched his face from brow to chin with a red ballpoint pen. It was quite shocking: during this righteous outburst of anger, Bubble Gum did not move a single muscle of his face, smiling non-stop. Stupefied, Father Augusto threw himself at him and, dealing him a real slap, shouted that he could no longer bear that damned "sarcastic smile." This understandably caused his complete disillusionment and was the last drop that emptied all of Bubble Gum's efforts to be loved. This disillusionment was so profound that his beloved Rector immediately banished him from the classroom. Bubble Gum left the room slowly, still smiling. He crossed the central corridor with a smile and twenty minutes later, during the 9:50 p.m. recess, was seen smiling at the top of the chapel tower. In fact, the older ones only noticed him because, in addition to smiling, Bubble Gum began singing a song that in his view perfectly expressed the spirit of his campaign for the Sanctification by Smile.

Which song was this?

Something very popular at the time. In and out of tune but with a clear voice, he delivered word for word the complete lyrics that have never left my memory: "A song of love is a sad song. Hi-Lili, Hi-Lili, Hi-Lo. A song of love is a song of woe. Don't ask me how I know. A song of love is a sad song. For I have loved and it's so. I sit at the window and watch the rain. Hi-Lili, Hi-Lili, Hi-Lo. Tomorrow, I'll probably love again. Hi-Lili, Hi-Lili, Hi-Lo. A song of love is a sad song. For I have loved and it's so. I sit at the window and watch the rain. Hi-Lili, Hi-Lili, Hi-Lo. Tomorrow, I'll probably love again. Hi-Lili, Hi-Lili, Hi-Lo."[2] After that, Jaguar-Bubble Gum burst into an embarrassing torrent of tears, and, sadder than he had ever looked before, took a resolute step into the air. The Rector, who was experienced in adolescent love, had already arranged for a group of strong boys to reach the top of the tower at the right moment and grab Bubble Gum, preventing him from diving into his well of despair. For months, the whole community commented endlessly on the failure of the Order of the Smile—snickering mostly, truth be told. Bubble Gum spent a few days at his parents' house to rest. And the door leading to the chapel tower remained from then on firmly locked to prevent other manifestations of love, like those we will see further on in various levels of detail.

Which of the two superiors was more important, more powerful, or wiser?

At first, they were nebulously equal, because they were equally superior. But, despite the difficulties of compar-

---

2 "Hi-Lili, Hi-Lo" song by Bronislau Kaper and lyrics by Helen Deutsch, 1952 (film Lili)

ing them on this level, it must be admitted that they differed widely. It is also true that their differences were kept as guarded as possible in order to not undermine their most holy unity in public. It was said, for example, that both earnestly discussed the Jaguar-Bubble-Gum case, which made their disagreements about educational methods quite clear and commonly known. Father Marinho found the Rector very severe. And Father Augusto found the Spiritual Director too accommodating. But in fact, there was a deeper-lying dispute between them, based on their different personal tastes and styles.

Which two temperaments did they represent, individually?

The mystical. The scientific.

In which other aspects did they differ?

Father Marinho devoted himself to the younger ones, while Father Augusto preferred the older ones. While the Mystic captivated with a beauty that was inseparable from his tenderness, the Rector's virile beauty entranced the teenagers. It would not be an exaggeration to speak of a mother and a father. Father Augusto, for instance, mostly concerned himself with the bodies and character of the boys. In his monthly lectures, he frequently referred to discipline as an instrument for forging men with a capital M, and by that he meant "masculine men." He clearly expressed dislike for the boys who were too delicate, and he despised the sissies, who, for obvious reasons, preferred the Spiritual Director, even when they were already in the older group. Against all mannerisms, the Rector severely criticized the habit of putting brilliantine in one's hair as an act of extreme vanity that did not suit manly behavior—though clearly, he was not entirely familiar with the hairstyles of Elvis Presley, a great worldly idol of the time. Evidently, such suspicions applied to the figure of Father Confessor, a good-natured old man who, in addition to a runny nose, liked to comb his hair in a style somewhat akin to Rodolfo Valentino, who also worshiped brilliantine. The Rector's concern with the boys' virility led him to extreme attitudes, as in the case of one of his favorites, Toady, whom he forced to fast on an ox blood diet every morning for two months in order to "strengthen the blood and the temper," he said. For him, after all, the body shaped character. Hence his very special care for the physical development of the adolescents.

How was this care manifested?

Just before bedtime, Father Augusto summoned the boys individually to his room—a maximum of three each night, in alphabetical order. There, he ordered them to take off their clothes and vigorously examined them to check their health and to make sure they followed the rules of hygiene that he prescribed. During one of these examinations, he discovered a genital infection due to poor cleaning. Thence, he went to great lengths to teach the boys how to lower the foreskin of their genitals and wash them with soap without fear of losing their virility. He did all this with extreme objectivity, but his professional gestures could not hide underlying intentions that the more sensitive students grasped. It was not uncommon for the examinations to end with the young members' unrepressed erections, excited by the warm and experienced touch of their beloved Rector.

Was there any more explicit sign of arousal on the part of the Rector?

Not much was known about this. It was indisputable—because undisguised—that he was attracted to the smell of teenage bodies. He prowled around them like a bullfighter prancing in circles, sniffing them subtly and slowly approaching until he hypnotically controlled his objects of analysis, his contenders, or his playmates. This was as part of the examination, but he couldn't hide the amorous impulse that entered his body via the nostrils. For his little fish the treatment had to be special. They said that he handled them in a more relaxed way and in some cases covered them with tiny kisses that were only slightly awkward, and that was how he enjoyed extracting veiled groans—a subtle and eloquent evidence of his mastery. However, none of this could be confirmed. The little fish, with rare exceptions, kept their secrets as a proof of their love. Most of the rumors that circulated in the cliques were connected to the Spiritual Director. But it was never clear where within these four walls the facts ended and where the fanciful additions of neglected teenagers consumed with jealousy began.

Was the desire for contact with the mystery of authority so deep?

It was as deep as is imaginable: stakes driving through the foundations of those loves in the making, undermining even the most resistant. There were teenagers who entered a state of panic in the days preceding their turn to be inspected. Panic, of course, was part of the magic: the teenagers trembled with the dance of the seducer. A siren inside them went off when they sensed even from afar that the Rector's nostrils were inflating, proof that they were capable of jolting and calling to themselves the passion of God. They experienced chills and waves of heat, not only of the flesh or the spirit: it wasn't clear which territories love had invaded. All the boys felt the presence of a tactile, strong, and protective Lord, so immeasurable that He would not fit, not even in joining their hands together, or in anxious kissing. They were enveloped in a wave of interchanged vibrations, lost in a space where angels soared beyond the boundaries. It was then that in an uncontrollable movement their cocks left the warmth of their recently born, fresh pubic hairs and levitated in pure ecstasy at the beginning of the examination.

And what did the Rector say to this not so subtle mystical propension that erected the flesh?

He interrupted the ecstasy with indirect reprimands—"don't you wash your member properly, boy?" or "you have to do more exercise to thicken those thighs." But he never alluded to the fact itself—the member's rigidity—because even if he did not approve of the means, he enjoyed the result. And this could be seen in the unusual brightness beaming from his eyes when young desires displayed their war cries, and new levers intervened in the movement of the world.

Why is it said that the Rector did not approve the means?

Because there was mystical worship in those hard cocks. And the mystical was the exclusive domain of the Spiritual Director.

So could it only be Spiritual if it was Mystical?

No. Also because the Rector never failed to refer to transcendence. But with his Apollonian predilections, he could never be a mystic. As for masturbation, which continued to be strictly controlled, the Rector thus expressed his view during the inspections: "Let me see your chest. Ah, a swollen chest. Too much masturbation, boy. See if you can get a grip. A swollen chest in a man is unseemly." The Spiritual Director was different: he engaged and took care of the younger ones as if already levitating and calling them up there with him. He used poetic stratagems: in the case of masturbation, he tied ribbons of various colors to the genitals of young reoffenders. The various colors corresponded to the severity of the masturbatory phases. A control mechanism that he personally and rigorously administered was to make the boys tie a knot in the ribbon with each new masturbation. Thus, he closely observed the sinful activity of the little ones, with a lot of imagination. And if he punished them, it was to uplift their spirit. When caressing his subjects, he was careful not to disturb them inwardly. He shook hands with one, stroked the face of another, and on occasion even touched them in manners that seemed more daring. In such cases, he immediately reassured them with convincing explanations. He alluded to the phrase that he had had inscribed above his door: UBI CARITAS ET AMOR, DEUS IBI EST ("Where there is charity and love, there is God"). Or he would put the boy on his knee and clarify to him in the sweetest way: "If there is true charity between the two of us, God will be with us." When, during spiritual consultation, the boys would tell him scabrous things, he would put them on their knees on top of the chair ("so that, when rising up, they can better ask God for forgiveness"), and while they were praying he touched their feet with his lips, delicately. And he explained: "It is in the name of compassion for our sins that the gesture of Christ's love at the Last Supper is repeated here." Gradually, his light touching with the lips took the form of explicit kisses that never lacked in tenderness and that bathed the feet of the small penitents. The characteristics of his relationships with the students were even more diverse than those of the Rector, especially considering the frankly ludic content of the arrangements.

What are some other examples of this ludic content?

Father Marinho had a stamp with the flaming Heart of Jesus. He liked to stamp the boys' chests right at the height of their heart, "So that their hearts burn in the love of Christ," he said. At recess, the older ones made fun of the younger ones: "Have you been stamped yet today?" Father Marinho did not care, because he knew the profound meaning of his games. He gave out delicate statuettes in beautiful colors to the boys who managed to overcome the temptations of the flesh. They were invariably images of Jesus caressing little boys, or embracing them in a protective gesture.

Wasn't this a rather bizarre form of love?

Yes. Looking at it from a distance, it was a perhaps bizarre form of love, but one that Father Marinho required unconditionally; he proposed, for example, that children speak directly to Jesus in their diaries. He encouraged them to write every day, beginning like this: "Dear Jesus." As an embodied representative of Jesus, he had direct access to the diaries, which helped him "to know the little souls better, in order to better direct them onto the path of Love." It is true that some seminarians would rebel against this in the more confidential moments of their lives, as we will see below was the case of Tiquinho. But it cannot be denied that such intimacy made Father Marinho's presence in the boys' inner life truly striking. At the intellectual level, he tried to instill in them a taste for music and literature. In his room, he organized musical auditions that were also frequented by many older students, and there he introduced the boys to the universe of Bach, Beethoven, and Brahms, "the most holy trinity of B's," he said. During recess, he used to place amplifiers on his bedroom window, so that the whole community would hear his collection of classics—then played in alphabetical order, which was to "clean up the most forgotten albums." In fact, at his insistence the students went to sleep and awoke to the sound of music—gentle sounds at night, and more vibrant music in the morning, transmitted through two loudspeakers that were installed in the inner courtyard that opened onto the dormitories. It was thanks to him that Tiquinho fell in love with Beethoven's Seventh Symphony—a composition that was received with indifference at its premiere in Vienna and that thence became the most misprized because it was so different from his other symphonies, Father Marinho explained. And he added: "In this case, difference is like a slightly non-standard season-ing, which adds a special charm because it breaks the perfectionism of the Fifth and Sixth." He argued that Beethoven was not clearheaded in the Seventh—a symphony of unclear and heterogenous spiritual sensations, and very perplexed, because Beethoven was in love when he composed it.

It is said that, besides causing fascination, music also allowed the expression of indefinable adolescent emotions. How did this work?

Very peculiarly, actually. The compositions, especially when they were played to sleep and wake up, functioned as stimuli that acquired specific emotional connotations, putting in motion the interior life of the children, not unlike how strong food puts the intestines in motion. Looking back, it would seem that the Superiors selected these recordings to control the feelings of the whole community and to mold their hearts like softened wax. If in this sense one could compare the priests to wizards, it is because in the evening hours especially the music brought to light an anonymous and diffuse sensuality, immersing the spirits in an atmosphere of pagan feast, in which fluid fantasies emerged suddenly, like palpable spells on bodies. It was not incidental that during this magical time both the Rector and the Spiritual Director received the seminarians in their rooms. Perhaps because music was a sister of poetry and a daughter of sadness, as Father Marinho frequently said, quoting some composer. At night, the perfectly rounded choirs of Verdi's operas gave rise to a respectable and placid romanticism, which inclined the little ones to an almost peaceful melancholy. Listening to Schubert's "Unfinished Symphony," the romantic imagination galloped with hearts drenched in the sweetest chords of the composition's opening and with emotions fueled by the mournful melody of the second part. In the morning, there were mischievous smiles when the "Nutcracker Suite" was played. But the expressions became grave when the morning music was Beethoven's Fifth Symphony. The "Brandenburg Concerts" caused a restrained lightness and an innocent euphoria when the flutes trilled. Tiquinho, in turn, felt delicious shivers ascending and descending his back, when in the mornings he heard the "Rite of Spring." But he was restless and had ponderous dreams after hearing Brahms's Symphony No. 3, which enveloped his spirit in damp shadows, with a swirling mist from which the shapes of ghosts emerged now and again. Later, after the dawn of a new love, music would become even more prominent in his universe: in the swelling of violins, in the movement of the horns and trumpets, or in the piano and violin solos, he would then find no less than the timbres, modulations, and cadences of his own passion. As an adolescent, he would discover that desire before all else is musical.

In addition to selecting books and guiding their reading, did Father Marinho not also organize literary contests?

Yes, he organized poetry recitation contests. In one of those, Tiquinho recited Jorge de Lima ("The World of the Impossible Boy"), scandalizing an audience accustomed to the grandiloquent discourses of Bilac, Coelho Neto, Castro Alves ("God, O God, where are you that you don't answer?") and Martins Fontes. It is worth mentioning that, thanks to the efforts of Father Marinho, he established himself as the most brilliant interpreter of modern poems in the Seminary, and received a number of successive prizes (a box with luxury envelopes, a book of poems by Michel Quoist, a short biography of Saint John of the Cross, and *The Little Prince*, which would mark his life, as we will see). Father Marinho also liked to direct theatrical works: "Tarcísio, Martyr of the Eucharist" with the younger ones and, with the older ones, "Ascent through the dark night," a minstrel play in which Saint Teresa converses with Saint John of the Cross on the topic of the Perfect Union between the Soul and her Spouse, Jesus Christ. It was this climate of intellectual stimulation that for the children eased the ascetic-mystical radicalism of Father Marinho. Because, unlike the handsome Father Augusto, he had no favorites; he treated everyone as if he were a delicate mother, without discriminating against overweight boys, or excessively pimply-faced ones, or awkwardly effeminate boys who were a laughingstock for many.

Famous were his visits to the sick in the infirmary, where he spent hours telling stories of Christian saints, Greek sagas, and Mayan priests—three different ways to sacralize the world, he said. This unconditional love created a kind of connivance between his followers, who tended to form a group more distant from the Rector and less focused on sports. Faced with the problems that such circumstances might create, Father Marinho remained unperturbed. When once the Rector burst into his room and in front of everyone sarcastically protested the absence of "the mystics" during sports, he replied without raising his eyes from the book he was reading: "For my part, I find it regrettable that your Apollos can never have access to the sports of the soul. As a matter of fact, we are in a Seminary, not in a physical education school." That was all he said.

What was the children's love towards him like?

At the same time passionate and naive. They loved him with an ambiguous fascination, because it was suffused with confidence and respect, but also with intense sensuality. There was in his room, always packed with boys, an atmosphere of rare physical closeness and emotional relaxation, as if many disciplinary rules had been inexplicably suspended and there was no strict timetable. Unlike on the soccer field, in here affection was not based on concealment. It was above all a generous space, where many could take refuge. Something undefined certainly was in the air, as if suddenly some invisible door was going to open to another world. In fact, the feeling of living in a different world was highly present in those hearts that began to discover unwonted passions and found, right there, a space that began to give these nebulous passions—for classmates, for God, for music, for nature, for life—some definition. For at that age everything is passion.

Was Father Marinho a kind of Socrates?

Socratic and Catholic, yes. Perhaps a mystical Socrates, who assuaged his own torments by surrounding himself with boys and loving them almost without limits, in fantasy. In fact, his communication with them revealed the extent to which they satisfied him. Before going to sleep—which for him was the most inspiring time, "because in the darkness God is closer"—he liked to gather small groups for what he called "Meditations of the dark night" and then commented on the Gospel of Saint John ("the one who found peace in the bosom of the Lord Jesus") and on poems from his beloved St. John of the Cross, as well as on passages from the Old Testament and almost pagan passages from the *Song of Songs*—the ones that fascinated Tiquinho the most. According to the Spiritual Director, the Gospel of Saint John was one of tenderness and transparency; he used to say that this "love with his head against his chest" was radical and had made the evangelist John a visionary; out of that love had been born the prophetic dreams of the Apocalypse, a deliriously mystical journey in search of the Beloved. As for the Old Testament, he had a strong preference for two passages that he frequently commented on during the Meditations: the struggle between Jacob and the Angel, and the near-immolation of Isaac by his father Abraham as an offering to God. The first passage spoke of man struggling with God, an impossible struggle in which the insignificant overcomes the Absolute. Father Marinho thought it sublime that the Greater Love of God ended by yielding upon recognizing the reflection of His greatness in man. On the other hand, the episode of Abraham, who in order to prove his love for God offers him his only son in sacrifice, brought Father Marinho almost to tears. God too must have been moved by the unconditional love of his servant Abraham. For in matters of Love only radicalism matters, he said in a small voice.

Was Tiquinho engaged in these spiritual wanderings?

Although he already belonged to the older group, Tiquinho attended the Meditations in the Spiritual Director's room for a long time. Not infrequently, he had the feeling that he was advancing in the discovery of a new spiritual continent. On one occasion, he left the room almost levitating, after hearing the words of Father Marinho, who that night had seemed to him larger than himself, as if he were two in one. The priest spoke of the tension between the morality of Christianity and its most mystical aspect, precisely because mysticism goes beyond the moral rules of everyday life and ascends to a higher level. The insistent death wish of Saint Teresa ("I die because I don't die") can be shocking to moralists, he said. And yet, real life can only flourish when unrestricted absolute love is possible. It is not by chance that Saint Teresa and Saint John of the Cross thought a lot about eternal resurrection of the flesh: they wanted to die in finitude to be resurrected in eternity and to be united bodily to the spirit of God. So, flesh and spirit would become one. Because everything started in solitude, said Father Marinho. The desire to sensualize the spirit and the consciousness of God as a whole may have existed in the human mind from the moment that man perceived himself alone.

Wouldn't these mystical elucubrations be too abstract for the children?

Yes, for many of them, who ended up sleeping, sometimes next to the priest. In any case, it mattered to him that some eyes shone more and more brightly as he communicated his visions to them, which they ingested like deliciously sweet seeds. Proof of this is that Tiquinho, for instance, never forgot those words and is still able to repeat them today. He heard—with all channels open—the explanation that, in renouncing himself to merge with God, man became everything, because he was immersed in absolute Love. Taken to its ultimate consequences, love for God could only bring about a form of madness, which mystics poured out in moments of ecstasy—when they loved, loved and only loved. And it was like a golden culmination when Father Marinho, before ending the Meditation, said: "It is necessary to love God, who is present in the other. If we all love each other like this, we will be one great mystical body. We will all be in Christ. We will be God loving Himself. Only this radical love can save us from madness." Later, whenever he wondered about the mysteries of love bursting in himself, Tiquinho would ruminate on those words—to understand more and suffer less.

At certain times, wouldn't Tiquinho be moved to bring music and mysticism closer together?

Yes. He was experiencing decidedly weird sensations. The "Overture 1812," for example, to him seemed to represent the struggle between Jacob and the Angel. He heard in it a succession of blows and counterblows, human blood combining with divine blood in Tchaikovsky's chords, until the end when, by virtue of commemorative bells and explosions, the spatters of blood transformed into the blazing veins of the sun, with man proclaimed victorious by God Himself. This is what my memory has retained.

A rivalry between the two superiors was mentioned. What were the terms of this rivalry?

It often went beyond the limits of authority. For example, some boys of the fourth year who were very close to the Rector commented that Father Marinho would have been expelled from the Order of the Carmelites as a seminarian, because of his special friendship with a colleague. This sounded scandalous and was clearly said with derision. Undoubtedly, it was part of the subterranean (but not always muffled) war that the two priests ended up waging among themselves. As a matter of fact, they often accused each other, indirectly, in front of the students. The Rector, for instance, in one of his lectures, characterized the devil as a blond and profoundly delicate being who seduced with his sweet manners. In his Meditations, Father Marinho retaliated by stating that the devil, contrary to what was commonly believed, was very beautiful, very manly, very martial, and loved to fight, but out of cowardice launched intrigues and slanders. The wicked explanation that the Rector only wore glasses to see less, appears to have been his own. Although he could not prove it, Father Marinho distrusted that too-sharp vision as something of the devil. He feared it as much as the fulminating beauty of the Rector, who in turn shuddered at the intelligence of the Spiritual Director.

It was said that Father Marinho was tormented. Was this pain mystical?

Yes, presumably a mysticism of the flesh. Father Marinho claimed that mystics were among the devil's favorite targets. He constantly referred to the physical and spiritual torments of Saint Teresa to try to console himself. But he certainly did not only comfort himself intellectually. They said that inside a closet that was always locked he kept cilices of various kinds, to tie around his waist and thighs. Cilices that were described in horrendous color, full of nails and sharp objects. True or not, on some mornings you could hear vague sounds of lashes coming from his room. Or sobbing, though this was unconcealed. Father Marinho was a man who wept. Everybody knew this, and he made no attempt to hide it. That's why so many boys cried in his room during spiritual supervision. Boys who were sad, tense, or simply in love, boys to whom, between caresses, he said: Blessed are those who cry, for the gift of tears is precious.

You mentioned that mystical experience was the exclusive domain of the Spiritual Director. What does the mystical have to do with a love that, like a hallucination, cannot contain itself within the limits of the spirit?

Perhaps the delights of the flesh are not necessarily opposed to the salvation of the soul. And this seems to be an acceptable conclusion in Father Marinho's mystical universe. In his view, mystics had an exceptional sensitivity that would lead them to traverse the territory of the flesh and overcome it—not in the sense of repudiation, but of re-dimensioning it. Because of their great capacity for love and passion, they would violate the flesh, aiming less at destroying it than at destroying its barriers and putting it back into the orbit of the spirit. It would be the universe of the purest flesh, as before the sin of Adam and Eve: an attempt to break away from history by immersing the body in eternity. These images, though grasped only nebulously, enchanted Tiquinho, because they projected love as an absolute, unlimited territory. And they ended up shaping his life, as we will see.

Yes, yes. There clearly is a story here. This will be shown.

Of the Carnalization
of Heaven and its Nuances

The boy Tiquinho seemed to experience everything in a single impulse. How did the call of the flesh begin to interfere with the call of God?

When still in his first year at the Seminary, Tiquinho almost drowned when a wave caught him off guard during on one of the communal walks on the beach. He was saved by a fellow student of the older group, who carried him in his arms to the sand, almost unconscious, gasping for breath and with panic-stricken eyes. While carried, Tiquinho felt the warm closeness of his rescuer's chest and sank his head into its abundant tangle of hair. The feeling of protection was unforgettable but not unique. While those strong arms supported him, he dreamt in his near fainting that he would never be lowered to the ground and wished for this as far as his desire could reach. Because the call was more complex, stronger. The hairs had a smell; the strong chest delivered comfort. The skin of the arms that enveloped him provoked delights whose signs Tiquinho had perfectly grasped long before. But now was the first time that he felt his flesh move uneasily, unmistakably, for the love of men.

Although sensitive to the male erotic appeal, can it be said that Tiquinho was naïve in the domain of carnal knowledge?

The newcomer Tiquinho was naïve to the point of being astonished by the first spontaneous activities of his own sexual mechanism. He didn't understand why, one morning, he woke up soiled, sporting a huge stain on his pajama pants. He began to be alarmed by the repetition of this to him inexplicable fact, and he did not know where to inquire. He didn't yet have the level of intimacy he would come to have with those who would later be his friends in the Flock. But he was only truly alarmed when, shortly afterwards, rubbing himself with soap while bathing, he had an unexpected erection, soon followed by butterflies in his stomach and a sticky squirt. Intuitively, he feared that it had to do with sin. He ran to the old Spiritual Director and only learned that he should rub less, so as not to provoke manifestations of the restless flesh, which easily led to sin against chastity. From then on, he lived in distress every time he bathed. But he forcefully remembered the strange satisfaction that he felt after waking up in a blur from dreams in which he plunged into an abyss as if flying, and it was there that he experienced the unusual pleasure of someone producing a less enduring and more profound pee, which was not pee, but released that cream that he soon learned to call spunk. Under the shower, he couldn't resist and rubbed his cock with his hands; as soon as he received the hot stream, he looked at his own sperm as Cain would have looked at the blood of his murdered brother, and again ran to the Spiritual Director, where he confessed and was again advised to escape the temptations of the flesh. But the yearning for satisfaction was greater than his will to restrain himself. Repressing himself to the limit and fearing the flames of hell, he was in fact obsessed with the idea of ejecting his fiery jet. In order not to sin, he invented a ploy in which he would not use his hands. He kept jumping under the shower, with the member hitting him in the belly, until he ejaculated. Even so, he ran heaving to the Spiritual Director's room and arrived saying: "Father, I was not pure in my actions." As a penance, the priest once recommended that he copy by hand the entire booklet The Pearl of Virtues. Tiquinho gladly did his penance. But the beautiful words in the book, which gilded chastity with a truly convincing brilliance, also had the effect of making the corresponding sin more attractive, which resulted in it being practiced with even greater insistence. Tiquinho lived immersed in dark feelings of guilt, making visits to the former Spiritual Director's room at least once a day to ask for absolution for his delicious mortal sin. It was no doubt thence that his early ascetic-mystical inclinations came into being, which would flourish in an almost poetic manner with the arrival of Father Marinho. I can still recreate in memory the strange atmosphere of these penances and spiritual outbursts. Tiquinho passed from sin to repentance in the same state of euphoria, and from there to compulsory sanctification. He also considered becoming a missionary. But he was most interested in giving up his life up for his faith, and dreamt of being martyred by pagans. With real conviction, he followed attentively the daily passages from the Roman Martyrology that were read during the final minutes of the evening meal.

What was so enthralling about the Martyrology?

It commemorated the saints of each day and recounted the torments they had endured in the name of the Christian faith. Tiquinho thought it beautiful to suffer for the love of Jesus. Like Saint Mark and Marcellin, who, persecuted by the Emperor Diocletian, were arrested and tied to a log, and had their feet pierced with sharp nails; but since they did not cease to praise Christ, their executioners stabbed their sides with spears. On the same day, Saint Etherius, who was beheaded after undergoing fire and other torments. And the passion of Saint Felix of Valois, condemned to death under the emperors Diocletian and Maximillian after being tortured on the rack. And the holy martyrs Hypatius and Andrew, who were beheaded, but first had their beards greased with pitch and burned, and their scalps ripped off. And Saint Pontian from Sardinia, who was clubbed to death by order of Emperor Alexander. And the blessed Calepodius, who was beheaded and had his body dragged through the city by order of Emperor Alexander, together with forty-two other persons, whose heads were hung on different gates of the city. Tiquinho listened with eyes wide open. And in the chapel, he asked God to allow him the glory of the most painful martyrdom, in order to prove how immense his love was for Jesus Christ. The following day, he listened tirelessly to the Martyrology, which told the story of the lives of the holy brothers Nereus and Achilles, who suffered the most severe flagellation and underwent torture on the rack and by fire; refusing to sacrifice their religious idols, they were finally beheaded. And even more to the life of Saint Corona, who to Tiquinho's delight was torn apart between two trees—limbs outstretched in love of Christ. And Saint Simplicius, pierced by a spear in the days of Emperor Diocletian. And the blessed Isidorius, who was thrown into a well which to this day makes the sick recover their health when they drink from its water. And Tiquinho marveled at Saint Dymphna, virgin and martyr, who was beheaded by her own father's orders, for being unshakable in her faith in Christ and in guarding her virginity. And also, Saint Restituta, placed in a tiny boat full of pitch and burlap that was set on fire, but the flames had turned against her torturers.

And Tiquinho listened and brooded over the pain patiently endured by Saint Dioscorus, who had his nails removed and was burned on his sides with lighted torches, and who was finally scorched with smoldering blades before he died. Or Saint Alexandra's torment, sunk in a pond with a stone around her neck. Or Saint Ciriac, atrociously scourged by whips and thrown into a fire because of her Christian faith. And Saint Basila, who refused to marry a pagan nobleman, replying that she already had the King of Kings as her Husband, and was therefore stabbed with swords. And Saint Aquila, torn open with iron rakes for the cause of Christ, thus receiving the palm of martyrdom. Later in the chapel, Tiquinho spent a long time meditating on such endless love for Christ, a love beyond imagination. As in the case of Saint Basiliscus, whom they put in iron boots studded with burning tips and whom they finally beheaded and threw into a river. And Saint Cointa, who did not want to worship pagan idols and was therefore dragged with ropes through the city, until her body was in pieces. He could not forget the dear Saint Tarcisius, who as a child refused to give the Blessed Sacrament to the pagans and was beaten by them with sticks and stones until he died. On his own he read about the martyrdom of the handsome Saint Sebastian, commander of the first cohort of the emperor and who, confessing to love Christ, was tied and shot with an arrow by his own soldiers and finally beaten to death, receiving the palm of martyr-

dom. And so too many anonymous Holy Martyrs, like those
from Cappadocia, who succumbed with broken legs under
Emperor Diocletian, and others from Mesopotamia, suspended by their feet, asphyxiated with smoke and burned
over a slow fire. For the love of Christ, Tiquinho took advantage of his position as a mealtime helper and once sneaked
into the kitchen, where, under the pretext of waiting for a
cauldron for a soup of chayote, he stood next to the wood
stove to test the smoke and heat, for the true love of Christ.
And he felt what all these martyrs had endured, because
he could not endure five minutes of martyrdom—not least
because there were only delicate nuns, who in no way resembled torturers, and also because the seminarians began to
beat impatiently on the plates, waiting for their food. Longing for martyrdom as a proof of love for Jesus, Tiquinho
examined the instruments and types of torture mentioned
in the Martyrology: *caulete*—a plump and pointed stick that
was used to inflict impalement; impalement—ancient torture in which the martyr was poked with a stake through
the anus until he died; *catasta*—platform or grid to stretch
the martyrs; *cilice*—fabric made of goat hair or rough wool,
but in a figurative sense it means any object that covers the
body to mortify it; *chumbeira*—whip or flagellum, garnished
with balls or pieces of lead (not to be confused with the scorpion); *scorpion*—bristly and prickly stick, prepared for flagellation; *flog*—stick to flog the body, with a different outcome

than *spanking*, which was hitting with a *panca*, that is, with a thick stick or lever. Among them all, Tiquinho ended up choosing the cilice, seizing on the disposition of some of his friends of the Flock, who also liked to kneel down on corn and sleep with stones under their pillow.

Was Tiquinho's love for Jesus that intense?

Despite having quickly abandoned the use of cilices, which were too uncomfortable, Tiquinho loved with passion. But he did not know (and this disturbed him) the nature of love expressed by Jesus: love one another as I have loved you. What kind of love would that be? Would Jesus Christ love with the same severity as the old Superiors? In that case, why had he allowed the Apostle John to rest his head on his chest, if touching each other was prohibited? In what way did Jesus love the apostles, among whom St. John was "the one whom he loved the most?" And the apostles, how would they love their Master? Of course, with the arrival of Father Marinho, these questions were assuaged with some clarifications. But still, Tiquinho could not understand why Christian love did not go beyond words and remained purely theoretical. Hence, he started searching for his own specific form of concretization. Love for him was always intensely concrete: something sensuous and spilling outward, an incessant act, an urge for touch and reciprocity. This is why the image of Saint John's resting head on Jesus's chest appealed to him so much. And it was precisely the Gospel of Saint John that expressed this insistence on true love. Like when after the Resurrection Jesus asked Peter three times: "Do you love me?" And Peter replied three times: "Lord, you know that I love you." So the sagacious Tiquinho reasoned that in the Gospel it was not forbidden to say "I love you" to another man. If this happened between Jesus and his disciples, why then was it forbidden? These were things he never quite understood.

How did Tiquinho get nearer to Jesus?

With the help of Father Marinho, who advised him to write a diary addressed to Jesus. Therein Tiquinho confided (almost) everything and wanted to be a true friend to Jesus. At the time, he began to talk at length with Christ, in the chapel, during numerous spontaneous visits to the Blessed Sacrament. He addressing Him informally, as one does with a true friend. He looked at the Crucified One and carefully examined his bloodstained body. He thought for a long time about the painful wounds on his feet, knees, chest, hands, and head. And he offered the special prayer: "they pierced my hands and feet and counted all my bones." Sometimes, he was moved by the Lord's helplessness, hanging there with his body exposed, and he felt an urge to heal his wounds, cleanse his dark blood, embrace him in a gesture of consolation. He often wondered what Jesus's living body might have looked like. Hairy? Strong? Tall or short? Dark hair or chestnut brown?

And wasn't Jesus's cinematographic revelation right around that time?

Yes, at that time, when Tiquinho started his third year, a film was projected in the study hall that left a definitive impression on him. It was titled *The Spanish Gardener* and related a story of friendship between Nicholas, the young son of the English consul in Spain, and a lad who took care of the manor's garden and who began to take the boy on walks to his home, and invited him to eat among poor people. The consul, resentful and afraid that something might happen to his son, finally ordered that the gardener, who besides poor and good was also exquisitely handsome, be arrested. In the end, the gardener died while trying to escape from the police. And Nicholas fell mortally ill, calling out the gardener's name. When the film was over, Tiquinho had resolved his most crucial problems regarding the love of Jesus. Like the boy in the movie, he already had a concrete friend. That dark Spanish gardener, with sweet almond eyes, a broad chest, strong legs, and good, and capable of loving Nicholas to death, was everything he imagined his Jesus was like. The discovery (or revelation) of a corporeal, visible, and beautiful Jesus left him dizzy. Quite perturbed, he managed to sleep only when the roosters were already crowing. He conversed at length with his dark Jesus and with his eyes closed said: "Jesus, my Spanish gardener, how I love you!" From thereon, he only had to look at the door of the bedroom and saw Jesus, who came smiling in his direction, dressed in a light tunic or even in simple pants and shirt, to converse and caress his head. Tiquinho started to receive these visits every night and so consoled himself whenever he experienced "affective problems" for other boys and whenever he had a test in mathematics or Latin the following day. This is how he discovered—and fell in love with—Jesus. And in this way he managed to glimpse the love of the Gospel.

From then on Tiquinho became a particularly devout seminarian?

Particularly devout, for he even spent part of the recess in the chapel. Not only did he speak to Jesus; he also began to taste the atmosphere of mystery produced by the smell of incense. He looked around and found himself surrounded by large frightful faces to which he gave himself up.

What were these large frightful faces?

They were the saints in the chapel, heavy wooden images with immense faces and oversized bodies. Tiquinho felt watched from above and had shivers, almost of seduction, when he imagined himself surrounded by real saints in colorful garments, decorated with meticulous pleats. He closed his eyes and venerated this authority that didn't scare him, also because the saints' niches were surrounded by paintings of angels with generously unfurled wings—like Icarus, who languidly looked up to the heavens with their hands flung to their sides or raised sweetly, and their wings describing graceful curves in an almost mannerist fashion. They were beautiful angels, their faces pink and strong. If it were possible to fear the scowling figurehead of those saints, Tiquinho indecorously thought, these beautiful angels would take it upon themselves to quell the fear and plant trust. In the chapel, he at once breathed sanctity and sensuality, a combination of veneration and surrender, because everything was colors and lights, and those large bodies, painted or sculpted, in their expressions were revealed as vibrant, enveloping, bountiful, and even anxious at times. Thus, Tiquinho immersed himself in sacred beauty, with a soul open to his Spanish gardener, who had been cruelly crucified by mankind.

There appear to be many colors to this memory. Which colors were these?

The colors of sanctity, no doubt. The whole year was arranged around colors that changed according to the liturgical season. At the Seminary, life was invariably marked by colors that defined the natures of the passions and the seasons of the spirit. During Lent, a bitter and resentful God was dressed in purple and forced the whole community into penance and grief—to mark, of course, the end of the holidays and interrupt the cycle of sins and transgressions. After that came purgatory, in which all the chapel's saints were covered in the same grave, sickening color, until the Heavens opened to the glorious white of Easter—a sign of cleanliness, triumph, and joy. Then, the chapel's saints again revealed their ghoulish faces, with chins, jaws, and cheekbones protruding and conniving. During Pentecost, life was tinged red, because the Holy Spirit illuminated everything with its fiery color, its fiery glow that bathed the prophets and made them speak in strange tongues. Green was the color of normal days, when there was neither joy nor special pain, and one had the impression that breakfast was reheated—so regular everything appeared. Unusual was the frightening black of the requiem masses that warned the living about the Last Judgment and that appeased the irate parched dead, and of the Dies Irae—fortunately few and rare days, on which the seminarians left the chapel downcast and bent down under the fear of death, which would come without warning or mercy. It was therefore necessary to always be prepared, in a state of grace.

How did their Christian hearts react to these rites?

The liturgy mobilized their Christian hearts with joyous celebrations or plaintive commemorations. In both cases stimuli of pain and joy were discharged as exact responses to those emotions that followed a previously and firmly set plan. At the Seminary the boys got used to following the rhythm that was stipulated for them by God, with whom they talked through colors. In fact, precisely these external elements broke the routine. My memory retains, for example, the intense and sensual aura of sacredness that emanated during Rogations, in the course of the Ember Days. For three consecutive days, the gates of the Seminary were thrown wide open to let the procession move in the direction of the street and into the world. An acolyte headed the procession with the cross and was followed by two cantors, who carried lighted candles to make their way in the dark of early morning and who chanted in a limpid voice and with bone-dry zeal the Litany of All the Saints, calling on Saint Maria, Saint Joanne, and so many other inhabitants of Heaven to listen to the supplications of planet Earth. The seminarians, dressed in cassocks and surplices, responded on behalf of the creatures: "ora pro nobis." They also entreated, "Libera nos Domine." From the devil's lures and perpetual death, deliver us Lord—they all sang in unison.

Was the chanting excessive?

Yes, in the darkness just before dawn, their voices resounded through the streets of the world, like voices of stray angels. "Orate pro nobis, miserere nobis." Immense was the cohort of heavenly angels who accompanied them.

Heaven welcomed all of them in one democratic gesture, including those old ladies who joined on the way, attracted by the invasive and irresistible air of sanctity.

Did God show Himself in all His glory?

In those days, God seemed almost vainglorious about his glory, dragging along the small crowd of worshipers. The officiant came behind, representing all the pomp of God with majestic cloaks, whose colors varied in the growing daylight. After circulating through the neighboring streets, invading profane homes with their Gregorian chanting, the procession entered the chapel for mass. Tiquinho felt shivers and was nearly in tears, because his entreaties rose higher and higher, up towards the mystery, and put him in contact with a grandeur that he imagined he could not reach. Perhaps because he found the Litany of the Saints so beautiful, or perhaps it was because it was a time of magic that resonated with the passionate loves choked in those youthful hearts that Tiquinho was so moved.

Tiquinho seemed particularly susceptible to these sacred atmospheres. Is that why he so strongly identified with Father Marinho's radical mysticism?

Father Marinho suffered from this same susceptibility to the sacred rites, which he approached in a personal and poetic way. At Pentecost for example, he trained a group to present in several languages the phrase "God is love" to complement the official liturgy. In doing so, he interpreted in his own way the gift of tongues, which was said to be the work of the Holy Spirit. Tiquinho, who ardently wanted to understand the meaning of love, was thrilled by the demonstration of love's universal nature. The melody of the *Veni Creator*, a hymn in praise of the Holy Spirit, penetrated his heart and turned him inside out to the last fiber. He uttered each word of the invocation with heartfelt devotion. "Thou art the living source. The fire. Thou spreadest the seven gifts (and are propitious to passion). Thou art the finger of God (it burns). Turn on your light. Blow thy love into my heart. Make me mad with love, O Holy Dove. But have pity so that it doesn't burn me." And Tiquinho felt small, under the wings of the Creator's Spirit, the incendiary dove that carried in his beak the burning irresistible love that God had revealed to mankind with his death.

But wouldn't the most noteworthy liturgical event be Holy Week?

Unquestionably. The seminarians then lived through an atmosphere of exacerbated passion, with feelings that emerged because the mystery of love (the God who dies for love) made everything transparent and entered their pores, body and soul. Everywhere people were speaking in tongues—not as an imposition, but as a natural need to pour out one's inflated interior. This atmosphere reached its emotional culmination on Holy Thursday, the Day of the Institution of the Commandment of Love—we will later see the importance of this for Tiquinho. But it was on Friday that the world was covered with tragic tinctures and the air was still and calm—on the Day of the Great Death and therefore the Tragedy of Love. Deep then was not only the feeling of irrefutable imminence, but also of perplexity, more in the heart than in the spirit. They stood before a Love that was so great that it led to Death. Their little hearts jolted in confrontation with this reality that was precisely the culmination of all the mysteries: "How was it possible to love so much to the point that one desires death for love? And what kind of love was that?" an excited Tiquinho obstinately repeated. This was evident even without explanations, there before everyone's eyes, in the purple color and in the mournful words of the rite. In the small hours between Friday and Saturday, the seminarians took turns worshiping the dead Christ in groups. The mystery of the chapel exceeded the mystery of the dormitory and overtook everyone. The boys got up in silence to visit the Sacrificed Love. Tiquinho was moved by the tragic generosity of that night. He stood in the presence of his dead Jesus and gave in to a devotion that flowed in vibrating waves. He did not want to forsake Christ in his very hour of acute suffering. He knew that in two days all this seemingly failed love would win forever. But he understood the sensation, no less painful for being merely transitory, of Christ entirely alone in the face of death, abandoned by all the living. At dawn, while the others murmured sleepy prayers, he got up on tiptoes and went to the coffin, because he believed in a secret between himself and Jesus. Then, surrounded by the grave sensuality of the naked altars and by the discretion of the saints in purple, he lightly touched (shivering) the wounds of his Beloved, of his sacrificed Gardener, and kissed the most beloved wound, that of the spear on the chest, the fatal, the cruelest wound. This dead Jesus of love belonged only to him and it was up to him alone to heal those wounds, and he alone was able to share the pain of all the divine blood drained by love. In fact, he couldn't help feeling that the Beloved had died exclusively because he loved him, Tiquinho. As a matter of fact, it must be admitted: Tiquinho did not suffer on Good Friday. He experienced an ecstasy of passion, when he mysteriously comprehended that the pain of death communed with the glorification of love through a direct and necessary channel. He closed his eyes. His hands went over those wounds and examined them, to better read them, to understand them. And he imagined himself lying at rest on the body of this naked Christ. Soaked in his blood. From so much love Tiquinho felt like a saint. Levitated. And he did not know yet that a year later love would incarnate itself, irreversibly and as a curse.

Wouldn't Christ be moved by this passionate retribution?

Definitely, yes. Later, Father Marinho would understand Tiquinho's vocation for radical love and to some extent started to guide him. For example, he gave him a biography of Sister Elizabeth of the Trinity, a Carmelite disciple of Santa Teresa who was a great mystic. Tiquinho and the priest read almost concurrently about the revelations therein contained.

What revelations?

That to love was to free oneself absolutely from everything that was not God.

And what else?

That there was no more difference between feeling and not feeling, between enjoying and not enjoying. One did not know anything for sure.

And what other things?

That the silence of the will was paramount in love. Silence was the last phase of dilution in the love of God.

And what else?

That in between the Soul in Love and his Divine Spouse could stand NOTHING, NOTHING, NOTHING. NOTHING on their path. And on the mountain: NOTHING.

Why?

Because the silent soul (and lover) no longer differentiated things, since he went beyond everything to surrender to the Beloved and rest in him.

Wouldn't that be a Love of death?

Yes, precisely like the dark night of Saint John of the Cross, in which all bodily activity dies. Before the face of God, only absolute silence.

And did Tiquinho understand?

He was ecstatic about this idea of love that annihilates itself for love. He didn't understand. But he thought it was beautiful. In the chapel, he wondered how a love that hands over everything, till the very end, was possible. He cried with emotion, not knowing how to answer. But he wanted to love like that.

Didn't Tiquinho ever answer a mystical questionnaire?

Yes, Father Marinho showed him the questionnaire that Sister Elizabeth had answered after she entered the Carmelite convent. And Tiquinho adapted his own replies to those very questions.

In what did the ideal of holiness consist for him?

Living in love.

What is the fastest way to achieve it?
Love without reservation. Loving love.

Who was his favorite saint?
John, the disciple who rested on the heart of Christ.

What was his favorite virtue?
The pain of loving. Blessed is he who weeps, for he will smile in love.

How did he define the prayer?
As a union between one who is nothing with That which is everything.

What disposition would he like to have when he dies?
He would like to love more than ever, before falling into the arms of his Eternal Beloved.

What kind of martyrdom most appealed him?
Every kind, but above all suffering for love.

What name did he intend to have in Heaven?
John, the one who loved too much.

What was his motto?
My Beloved and I are one.

Of the Mystery of
the Holiest Person

And how does Abel Rebebel finally enter these remembrances?

Abel Rebebel enters the story on a windy day in early August, when Tiquinho was in his third year. Forever etched in memory are the dry leaves wildly swirling in the outer courtyard and on the soccer field, the excitement of the seminarians who had just returned from vacation, exchanging news while preparing the house for a new academic semester. They all had renegade hair and unkempt thoughts. Life was disheveled and wildly stirred before it would again be made to completely fit into the Regulations and be contained by monotonous schedules.

And how did Tiquinho come into Abel's story?

Right in the beginning. Indeed, in the very beginning. Perhaps because he was the best student in the class, Tiquinho was called to serve as an angel to a novice who had arrived out of season and would join his class group, after the Seminary where he studied for some reason had been closed. Tiquinho went up to the dormitory and sat on the edge of his bed, waiting for the new pupil to arrive. The window-panes were down and rocked with the force of the wind, almost thirty windows beating in uneven cadence like a fan-fare band drumming. Tiquinho stared at the floor, still long-ing for the holidays. When he looked up, by chance, he saw an amazing picture: framed by the doorway of the dormi-tory, the Spanish Gardener arrived with two heavy suit-cases, stepping over unsummoned into reality. Tiquinho took a few seconds to try to understand what was going on, not knowing whether he was supposed to smile or just wake up. He stood up. He stumbled when he tried to take a few steps forward. With his eyes fixed on that living image that crossed the bedroom to meet him, he waited for the moment when everything would fade away. But no. He again forced himself towards this vision that already had become too concrete. His legs were shaking when he faced his pupil. This was no vision, but without doubt a Spanish Gardener in the flesh. Seized by a sense of vertigo, Tiquinho leaned on the head of a bed to avoid falling over. He tried to speak. No voice. He surmised that he was having a nebulous, no doubt mystical revelation. He even thought of ecstasy. And he only returned to his senses when he heard the image ask, somewhat hesitantly: "Are you ... my angel?" He managed to stammer: "Yes." And the Gardener's voice became firmer: "I am Abel. Abel Rebebel. It's a funny name, half Spanish." The memory gets fuzzy at this point; so many feelings blended in Tiquinho's agitated heart. While leading Abel to his assigned bed and pointing out his closet, he stumbled so many times that he could easily have given the impression that he was lame or blind. In fact, his eyes strayed from Abel's face as if they feared the sight of God himself. He no longer had any doubt: he was faced with a revelation as stunning as ecstasy. He loved Abel from that first vision. And he surrendered to the hurricane that the month of August had foreshadowed.

What was the vision of Abel like?

Identical to the Spanish Gardener, now illuminated by daylight. A Jesus Christ with slightly almond-shaped eyes, very dark hair, a straight body, kind features, and a vigorous brightness in his look.

Was Abel older than Tiquinho?

Yes, by one year. He was fourteen then, but he looked much older because of his more developed size and physique.

Was Abel especially alluring?

Yes, because he added to the image of Spanish Gardener a combination of virility, grace, and skill that was revealed when he walked in his sensual stride.

And from then on, how did Tiquinho behave around him?

With uproar in every pore. He wanted to keep Abel's image for himself, to prevent his image from leaving his privileged gaze. After his initial bewilderment he became an exemplary angel. He incessantly accompanied Abel to the chapel, to the playground, to the cafeteria. And he explained everything about the new Seminary. As Abel came from a warmer region and had only brought light clothes in his trousseau, Tiquinho offered him his best sweater for the coldest nights. Since the sweater did not fit, Tiquinho brought one of his blankets and offered it to him. As soon as he discovered Abel's fondness for soccer he offered his widest pair of shorts that he had not yet worn. And he did not cease to offer him books, sweets, and fruits sent by his parents. He managed to lavish so much attention on the pupil—taking advantage of his privileged position as an angel—that they ended up studying together and became good friends. After all, they had a lot in common. Despite being a manly type and an excellent soccer player—he was immediately part of the Seminary's team—Abel was very fond of reading and proved a diligent student. As a result of his transfer he had been forced to repeat the previous year and so with no effort rose to the top of his class. In order not to lose his position—but also to match Abel—Tiquinho redoubled his efforts in studying. As a result, they became the best students of their class. This did not prevent them from continuing to study together, especially since Tiquinho did not feel in the least threatened. From the beginning he feared only that he might be rejected and lose the object of his fascination.

Wouldn't that unexpected incarnation of the Spanish Jesus-Gardener mark Tiquinho's life to the point of dominating him like a bird enchanted by a snake?

Abel was his magnet and compass. And Tiquinho's life took on an extraordinary brilliance from that revelation. With his gaze fixed on Abel, he bravely endured the most boring lessons. He also complained no longer about the study schedule after lunch, because he then took advantage of his sleepiness to daydream about Abel, and to pour his dreams into extravagant drawings in which Abel had undulating wings and caramelized eyes, and thighs more shapely than those of Samson.

Was Abel the center of his life?

Abel was life. When they diverged, even in ordinary situations, Tiquinho experienced a feeling close to death when sensing even minimal prospects of separation. Conversely, the daily contact with Abel and fulfilment of this friendship brought him a happiness almost greater than he could bear. At first, he didn't realize he was in love. But his diary became a detailed script of his passion. Afraid to reveal too much, he started preventing Father Marinho from reading the diary. Therein all his joys, concerns and thoughts about Abel were reported. He reported the delights of his daily encounters and his anxiousness about Abel's possible reactions to one or another stance he might have taken. He commented on his daydreams. About his romantic intentions with Abel. About his plans to always be closer. Or about how Abel had suffered mild diarrhea. And on how strange the city's climate was. How he missed a game of soccer and got bored. And how he had gotten a lower score for Portuguese, so that Tiquinho made haste to offer lessons on the history of grammar. And how Abel didn't feel pious enough. In the diary, Tiquinho already revealed a hint of anguish, a little blot in the impetuousness of his daily elations. There was a small fear that he might sin by manner of excess. He who wanted to possess was beginning to feel possessed by the miraculously incarnated Spanish Gardener.

How did Tiquinho manage to always sit next to Abel at the cafeteria tables?

First, under the pretext of his role as an angel. After this excuse was worn out, Tiquinho became friends with the Prefect in charge of the postings, and offered him gifts in exchange for the privileged place next to Abel—a fact that of course began to provoke rumors.

And how did Abel react to this siege?

Abel was willing. With extreme generosity. Among them, he was the one who let himself be conquered. This was his particular way of conquering, as soon will be revealed.

How did Tiquinho first describe Abel?

Tiquinho described Abel in a hardly veiled manner in a creative writing exercise for his Portuguese class. Informed by incoherent memories from the film *Blood and Sand* (with Tyrone Power), Tiquinho recounted the rise and glory of a small gardener named Pablo who became the greatest bullfighter in Spain. He got a 9.5. Half a point was taken away for what, according to the instructor, were excessively baroque and florid descriptions of the protagonist. In fact, the entire narrative served as a pretext to evoke Abel's figure under the svelte vestments of the bullfighter Pablo. It was such a subjective description that one could speak of Abel according to the gospel of João. There were many wanton details that only thinly disguised his true feelings—for example, mentioning the admirable piety with which Pablo prayed to the Virgin before entering the arena, and the fascination he wielded over all the women in the country. According to Tiquinho, this gardener—who had become Abel, who in turn had become Pablo—looked like this: he walked like a heron parading in front of a wild animal. The muscles of his thighs stretched with each stride like the strings of a tuned violin, and they undulated with the sweet melody of his body under clothes embroidered with silver threads. His legs were more solid than those of the contending bull, yet Pablo stood with the lightness of a mastiff ready to jump. His shoulders were broad like those of an Iberian Tarzan (and here, frankly, his exaggerated fantasy led Tiquinho to forget that the bullfighter's attire usually has padding on the shoulders). His soft-haired arms concealed under their robust muscles a strength impossible to imagine in a man only nineteen years old. (First: the arms of a bullfighter are not bare in the arena; second: it was necessary for Abel to look in full bloom, to shine at the height of his youth; after all, this was presumably a prophetic text.) His hands holding the red cape of the "torero" with incomparable art resembled those of a prince in their elegance and proportion. In Tiquinho's vision, Pablo's chest seemed invented by some Renaissance artist (though he couldn't think of a specific name) who had taken his most delicate brush to draw soft black hairs in the dividing valley between the two mountains of Apollo (forgetting once more that bullfighters don't fight in the nude). And then the face: the black hair shone in the evening light and was tied behind the neck, forming a delicate lock in the manner of a black rose. His ears, small and shapely, stood out slightly and resembled tiny wings. Although completely shaved, his beard seemed lush and gave a bluish tone to his chin and jaws. The outline of his nose was somewhat interrupted in the middle, calling to mind a boxer's. His lips were pink and moist. His jaws were firmly built, outlining near-straight angles that were nonetheless smooth. His chin had a dimple where a droplet of sweat sometimes came to rest. And the eyes ... Ah, his eyes defeated the bulls. They shone without fear, tempting, inviting the beholder to dive into their black wells. His eyes, topped by arched eyebrows, were the doors through which supplications entered, and from which javelins or banderillas were launched. In Tiquinho's text, Abel's eyes were presented as a final offer in which the writer poured his own sensations. Clearly, he described Abel from the point of view of a bull (himself), fragile and eager to surrender to a most wonderful form of death. Like all the women of Spain, the poor bull had fallen in love with the bullfighter.

Did Abel read the composition?

In class, the teacher read some passages aloud. Abel looked at Tiquinho with a look of perplexity that did not hide his flattery and complicity. Blushing, Tiquinho looked away from the black wells. In any case, later Abel came up to ask him whether Pablo was him. Tiquinho hesitated, gasped for air, and gave him a no with all the inflections of a yes. Then he abruptly turned around and left in a panic. He was no longer sure what territory he was entering.

What did Tiquinho do in the middle of the night?

In the middle of the night Tiquinho used to wake up, touched by passion. Then he would quietly rise and go to Abel's closet, where he would sink his face into the shirt Abel had worn during the day, inhaling for a long time an intense smell of sweat that filled him with delight. During the night, Tiquinho also relished taking Abel's underwear out of his laundry bag. He avidly smelled those spots stained with various colors and odors. Then he looked into every corner, looking for a hair that he could collect and safekeep in the middle of his Seminarian's Manual, to contemplate and touch whenever he missed him. But Tiquinho did not only search for tokens of Abel at night. When Abel got a haircut in the infirmary, he accompanied him with the pretext of getting his own hair cut, or healing an improvised wound, and stayed there until he managed to furtively grab a trimmed tuft of his gardener's hair. Then he kept it at the bottom of his study card, inside an *Adams Chiclet* box. Tiquinho also loved Abel's skin. When on sunny days the seminarians held their walks on the beach, shortly afterwards they would often strip naked and enjoy themselves scraping off pieces of skin that they would fling everywhere. Tiquinho then made special visits to the Holy Sacrament and knelt in the same place Abel usually did. While he did not disguise his ulterior motives before the Holy Sacrament, he was also honest enough not to include these visits in his

Spiritual Bouquets, since these were not sacred visits, but true archaeological expeditions in search of the skin that Abel would have shed there during his prayers. Tiquinho carefully looked around, on his knees, crouched and sitting. With infinite euphoria he collected pieces of Abel.

But what purpose would Abel's disposable skin serve?

For instance, Abel's skin could advantageously cover the entire surface of Tiquinho's skin—to protect himself with something so holy, or to regally adorn himself with Abel and be simply consumed with shivers. Abel's skin could also be used for body-to-body contact, placing it on the hair on his arms. Or on the face. Or on the eyes, thus covered with the most delicious of membranes, the one that blinds with love. With Abel's skin he could also seek the taste of his sweat and of more intimate subcutaneous flavors. Ergo, its uses were inexhaustible. Tiquinho kept it carefully between pieces of cotton to find new ways to use it the next day and the following, and for whenever he craved being closer to Abel and feeling almost inside Abel. Or else he saw it as a simple relic of Abel. At other times, he merely held up Abel's skin against the sun. Like this, he would watch the light pouring through Abel's enlarged pores, filling Abel with brightness. With Abel's skin, he not only could study Abel's anatomy, but also understand Abel's spiritual metabolism through photosynthesis and so, perhaps, reach Abel's ultimate origins. Because Abel was in the end a result of the combination of the body's salt and sunlight. Aided by his meticulous examinations of Abel's skin, Tiquinho wanted to unveil the miracle of Abel's existence. To better participate in it.

Did Tiquinho dream about Abel?

He dreamed with his eyes open. He imagined himself lost in the forest, surrounded by animals and enormous snakes. Then Abel appeared naked as Tarzan and saved him. As a sign of gratitude, Tiquinho gave him an entirely pure kiss. Abel reciprocated. But then Tiquinho was woken by the Prefect's bell at the end of the study period. And he sighed with such conviction that his eyes closed, like those of a little virgin.

Did Tiquinho also make anonymous gifts for Abel?

Not content with giving gifts directly, Tiquinho put a tangerine under Abel's plate in the cafeteria. Sometimes he left an apple hidden under his shirts in his closet. Or he left a beautiful card of a little saint inside his desk in the study hall. There was also candy in his shoes, boots, and slippers. Abel didn't complain. He accepted Tiquinho in silence.

And Abel's soccer shorts, how were they used?

Abel's shorts were the ones previously given by Tiquinho, who took them back one night, when they were already duly blessed and thoroughly drenched in the delicious sweat of Abel's groin which Tiquinho breathed in with closed eyes, emitting squeals of pleasure before wearing them every night under his pajamas. This was his way of sleeping with Abel.

How did Tiquinho experience Abel's sweat?

Like a mistletoe for his heart. That was how Tiquinho experienced the strong smell of Abel's sweat, which initially left large wet stains on his shirt (on the armpits and elsewhere) and after sedimentation acquired a slightly yellow tone that gave a color to the essence of Abel's perfume. Tiquinho could smell it from a distance and it was through his olfactory organ that his heart opened and irresistibly surrendered. He enjoyed approaching Abel after a game of soccer, or during the mandatory 12:30 p,m. work session. His nostrils would then inflate till they were nearly torn, and he wanted to tear them open for all the gardener's perfume to penetrate them. Tiquinho dreamed of bathing in Abel's sweat.

Couldn't we call this an obsessive love?

No. Simply because there is no love that is not obsession. Otherwise, how could we determine and elucidate the reasons why someone is specifically attracted to another and loves them passionately? Why is love so often a one-way bridge on which the delivered feelings are not reciprocated? And why, on the contrary, is it sometimes mysteriously reciprocated and the chemistry of happiness works? How can one understand these unknowns as anything other than a permanent obsession with breaking down the boundaries between the self and the other? What moves us towards the absolute gratuity of loving and being loved? Might it be the search for that other part that we lack, metaphysically speaking, because we are only born half, as Greek mythology argues? Might it be the search for the lost mother, as psychoanalysts suggest? Or an attempt to break with the world's indifference and to reconcile what we are with what we are not, as certain philosophers say? Is love an attempt to understand ourselves through the mirror of the other? Or a blatant inclination toward the absurd, a pure and deliciously elaborate mystery of nature that makes the impulse to reach beyond ourselves more decisive, relentless, and disturbing, imposing disorder on the world and on the loving spirits? Love, then, would be a terrific prank of a nature bored with the order of life, and we would be living an elaborate joke when we love. If in this domain nobody understands anything and there are only hypotheses, how then can we accuse Tiquinho of being obsessive? Tiquinho was simply acting out the mystery of love. In the most genuine way. In a flux of generosity that in his future life would be increasingly reduced as he developed defenses and formu-

las. In this very moment Tiquinho was blessed. A period of
sparkling privilege began in his life, with powers unleashed
that were unexplainable to any scientist, or even to him,
Tiquinho, who never tired of examining Abel's skin, his worn
clothes, the remnants of his hair and the wet stains that had
passed through his clothing, which were all concrete expressions of Abel's relationship with the world. Because he did
not find sufficient reason, Tiquinho submerged into obsession and remained there like a stuck record. There he ini-
tiated his experience with delirium, allowing himself to be
possessed by love as by God—or by a demon, depending on
the point of view and the circumstances. Without a doubt,
that Tiquinho is now remembered with nostalgia. And with
jealousy. This is the defense of Tiquinho's obsession. For in
this world delirium is necessary.

Is there a clear example of delirium in Tiquinho's love?

In addition to those already mentioned, Tiquinho used to
wander the soccer field with a wand and set about writing
his poem on the ground, perhaps inspired by Saint Anchieta. It was a poem with two unique words, which he wrote
repeatedly in bold letters. Abel Rebebel, and then a new
verse: Abel Rebebel. The soccer field would have been satu-
rated with this boundless expression of love if Canary did
not follow in Tiquinho's footsteps to erase the signs of his
delirium. With a branch of eucalyptus as a broom, his friend

Canary undid the inscribed words and, almost in a state of panic, repeated: "For the love of God, Tico. This is a private friendship. If the Rector finds out you will be expelled."

And Tiquinho?

He laughed crazily and reiterated—sometimes in a low voice, other times higher, depending on his spirit—all the syllables of his obsession before writing them down. As stated above, he was possessed. At that stage, the threat of expulsion did not restrain him, nor was Paradise gated. Paradise lived inside him and was present precisely in these delirious manifestations in which the passionate soul syntonized only with the object of his passion. Speaking of delirium—wasn't Anchieta delirious, writing sacred poems in the midst of cannibalistic pagans in a country that one could without exaggeration call "the end of the world"?

Would delirium not also lead to tears of pain?

To tears, yes. But in this case, the tears were not just caused by pain or happiness. Tiquinho cried simply out of love, which is different, because love means a spiritual dysfunction whose most immediate, most visible and wanton physiological result is to set in motion the tear glands. Tiquinho worried that he was not wanted. He worried that he wanted more than he was allowed. Sometimes he would run to the Spiritual Director's room and confused the reason of his tears with the emotion caused by the music. Other times he did not. In detail he explained to Father Marinho the sensations that he was experiencing. At first, the Father spoke to him about the beauty of great friendships. He even consoled Tiquinho by reading him several passages on biblical love. Including a small and unforgettable verse.

From Song of Songs, 5–8?
Exactly. And it goes as follows:

> *Daughters of Jerusalem, I charge you—*
> *if you find my beloved,*
> *what will you tell him?*
> *Tell him I am faint with love.*

It was very much the style of Father Marinho to be accommodating at first. In a mournful manner, he read entire passages from Saint Teresa of Ávila's comments on some especially ardent verses of the Song of Songs.

"Let the Lord kiss me with the kisses of His mouth, for His love is more delightful than wine!"
Yes. This is when she defends the right of the enamored Soul, in speaking of God, to use the same expressions as carnal lovers, because it is possible for the Soul to go through death, affliction, delight, and joy together with her

Spouse, after completely abandoning herself to divine tenderness. Calling God "His Majesty" and "my Divine King," she defends the Soul, claiming that everything is allowed to those who, due to their total love for the Lord, come to be besides themselves. At that point, Saint Teresa concludes, in ecstasy, by begging the Beloved to impart peace to her with a kiss on the mouth.

And Tiquinho?

He was so amazed that in his diary he started calling Abel "His Majesty" and "My Divine King."

And Father Marinho, how did he respond to Tiquinho's visceral interpretation of this mysticism or poetry?

Comprehending that another kind of drama was playing out in Tiquinho's heart, he became elusive and confused—perhaps even frightened. He listened with evident agitation and did not respond clearly to the boy's anxious questions about the mysteries of love. On the contrary, he turned in circles, avoiding dealing directly with the subject. He was no doubt on slippery ground. But Tiquinho appeared whimpering at his office so many times that one day Father Marinho was forced to face the situation and severely admonished him against the dangers of earthly ties, because Love with a capital L could be achieved—for everyone striving for perfection—only in the inexhaustible surrender to God, the only and true Beloved. Tiquinho was startled. For the first time, he had the feeling that he was facing a dangerous rival who had found an exclusive medium of expression in Father Marinho. He realized that now he had everything against him. At first, he tried to reconcile. He strove to overcome all earthly appeal and to love God with greater dedication. For some time, he even stopped his idyll with Abel and mortified his flesh. He again spent long hours in the chapel, meditating on the Resurrection of the Flesh, when, finally, he would be able to stay forever at Abel's side. But the result of so much meditation was that he came to the obvious conclusion that the Resurrection of the Flesh would take too long. In the meantime, there would be an eternity of distance between him and Abel—and this would be equivalent to exchanging a bounded Paradise for an endless hell. He refused to accept defeat. He discovered a theme that would become a constant in his inquiries and meditations in the months of restless passion that were approaching: a true miracle had happened and Jesus had indeed incarnated in Abel—hence they were both so beautiful, sweet, and physically similar. Not entirely without logic, he reasoned that the Resurrection of the Flesh happened every time Jesus appeared to him in the bodily form of Abel. If the concrete world shone so brightly with the presence of Abel, it was not necessary to seek perfection in a future as distant and uncertain as Eternity. Instead of entering into confrontation, Tiquinho preferred to bargain with God. Perhaps this explains why, from here on, his contact with the Spiritual Director began to diminish.

Did the transfiguration of the world through Abel become clear at specific moments in Tiquinho's life?

Yes. There were certainly moments in which God could do nothing, because he was abstract and ambiguous, and no longer meaningful in concrete situations. An example? What could God do to free Tiquinho from the Bottle Game that, despite Father Marinho's protests, continued to be practiced (albeit less frequently) in the evening recess? In this context God was so helpless that Tiquinho had already given up pleading for mercy and tried to protect himself on his own. But slight as he was, and perhaps because he became the object of subtle revanchism by classmates less advanced in their studies, he suffered constant and veritably collective attacks in the Bottle Game. One night, he was unfortunately cornered next to the columns of the outer courtyard, so far from the bottleneck that he received a beating of dried glue pellets for the entire half hour of recess. He leaned against a column, trying to protect his face with his arms raised, and there he stood like a little Saint Sebastian struck by his cruel soldiers. He cried, shouted, and asked for mercy while hit from all sides. And what happened that night? As if by magic, a corridor opened between the furious assailants and

Tiquinho, through the blurring interference of his tears, saw approaching the figure of the Spanish Gardener, who was neither a fantasy nor a miracle, but Abel himself. Distributing punches and elbows, Abel reached Tiquinho and pulled him up, to the booing of his assailants, who, however, did not dare strike him. Tiquinho cried with all the floodgates open. But the nature of his sobs was changing as Abel took him away. In the basement, next to the storage room, Abel embraced him. Time stood still, and Tiquinho began to cry with intense happiness, his head resting on Jesus's fragrant chest.

How would one define this meeting?

As a mystery. It can be said that the Mystery of the Most Holy Passion began to unfold there.

Of the the Uncertain Chords
of Rachmaninov

Did Abel really love Tiquinho?

Yes, Abel's love was real. To my memory, his love left a mark, although it was different from Tiquinho's unstoppable passion, whose heart was liquefied with joy. One can try to understand Abel's love as a gesture of availability that eventually led to generous surrender and, from there, to genuine affection in return for the love offered. At first glance, it would be easy to say that Abel was mostly in love with the passion that Tiquinho devoted to him. Perhaps his love had started there, but it no doubt continued opening its own paths. The truth is that Abel had a different sensibility that was more restrained and less obstinate. On the other hand, Abel easily overcame the sneaking scruples that worried Tiquinho. Abel loved more directly and more candidly, without asking too many questions, and in a more conventional way, as we shall see. In that sense, he was happier, even though he did not reach the unconditionality (and transfiguration) of Tiquinho's love. As a matter of fact, there is no point in comparing them. It is sufficient to say that Abel discovered Tiquinho's unquestionable love and that this touched him, opened the doors of his heart, and led him to discover unchartered territory within himself. Thanks to him, Abel opened up. His love for Tiquinho was even a manner of expressing gratitude.

How was Abel sure that Tiquinho loved him?

By secretly reading his diary. This was considered a grave act of disloyalty among the boys, as it meant taking possession of the other through his secrets—something that each tried to keep to themselves. Abel confessed to Tiquinho that he had been reading his diary for some time and had thus kept track of the anxious developments of his love for him. Tiquinho only outwardly felt invaded. Deep down, he had always wanted Abel to dare as he did. That to him sounded, first of all, like a blessing.

And what did Abel read that was so persuasive in Tiquinho's diary?

In addition to the daily reports about him, Abel found a long explanation that probably helped him to make sense of his love. Tiquinho's reasoning began with the mystery of the Holy Trinity, whose interpretation he sought in a poem by Saint John of the Cross, in which love intrinsically solidified the Three Persons. Here it is, almost with nails pinned to my memory:

"Like the beloved in the lover,
one in the other resided.
And such love that unites them
in the same coincided,
because one matched the other
in intensity and worth.
Three Persons and a loved one
among all three there was
only one love in them all
and a single lover united them,
in such an ineffable knot
to say it was not known.
the love that merged them
and of being so one love,
so much more love was there."
—St. John of the Cross

How did Tiquinho develop his reasoning?

Like this: "The Holy Trinity is one God united by one love. This one God dwells everywhere. In me and in Abel too. As Jesus is God, Jesus is in us. We are two, but we became one because of the presence of Jesus and his love. I love Abel as myself and the love of Jesus is the same within us. As such, our love is one. If Abel and I don't love each other, Jesus's love will be incomplete. But if we love each other, it will be a love for all eternity. Lovingly united in Jesus, Abel and I will never be apart."

Was Abel daunted by this?

It seems he was overawed as someone who receives an ultimatum.

How could Tiquinho be sure of Abel's love?

Because one night he woke up astounded when someone entered under his sheets. The astonishment turned to incalculable happiness when he sensed the familiar smell and warm proximity of Abel's body—a body hitherto only imagined, never touched. Tiquinho asked no questions, nor did Abel say anything as they embraced as one, like the Holy Trinity.

How long were they like that?

Nobody ever knew. Because their eternity presupposed, as is natural, absence of time.

Did they sleep beatifically?

No. They kept their eyes wide-open in the dark, working out each other's form and touching their bodies. Their hands were shaking, not from fear but from passion. On the one hand, they were committing sin. Doing so, they discovered delicacies that were so surprising they made them tremble, because in great delights all balance is lost. Tiquinho used his hands to complete his vision. He touched the adored thighs and the idolized chest. He caressed his raspy beard. Then he activated his sense of smell and inhaled the smells he had once probed through indirect means. Finally, this triggered his palate; he arduously wanted to know the taste of Abel's skin. And he gave him shy kisses on his face, neck, and chest, not daring to go deeper.

And Abel?

Abel alternated between immobility and uneasiness, evidently demonstrating the same loss of balance, the same uncertainty about the terrain to cover and which emotions to express. His hands firmly tightened around Tiquinho's small body. He embraced him, wanting him entirely for himself. And he grunted like a bull, undecided about the right time to lunge forward. These games evidently broke down the dams they each held within. Neither Tiquinho nor Abel realized how far they had gone in Christian love. From then on, they created an ineffable knot that was not possible to explain.

Why had Abel dared so much?

Probably because he couldn't withstand the curiosity to unravel the corridors of that love he had made out from a distance, in the pages of Tiquinho's diary. And because he wanted to traverse his own labyrinths.

And the following day, how did they feel?

Transfigured with passion. There was no shadow of remorse, but only a baroque desire to repeat it in almost narcissistic eruptions. The world was reduced to their desire to be together. And their iron discipline melted in the heat of their passion. They were incapable of anything besides looking for each other in every corner of the house and paying attention to the sound of their voices. Typical anxieties of lovers—only understood by those who have also played a part in dramas of passion.

How did they sate their desire?

Satisfaction was a vain utopia. But they allayed its absence in the chapel tower, where they spent their time hidden, hand in hand and eye to eye. There they read *The Little Prince* together, which they had just discovered. Abel read aloud, tirelessly fondling Tiquinho's hair, who surrendered like a lamb with curly wool. It was delightful to learn that each had captivated the other (captivate meant "bonding") and that they were uniquely destined for each other in this world. Of course, the tower's refuge lasted only until Bubblegum-Jaguar attempted suicide and Father Augusto thence deemed it prudent to keep the entry locked. Tiquinho and Abel finished reading the book in the eucalyptus grove and reread it more than once, always in the eucalyptus grove—a bit bold, because the community then witnessed the undisguised manifestation of their love, even though they held back. Gossip started to proliferate. But since the essentials remained invisible, the two did not care and proceeded now to read *The Little Prince* in French. They wanted to read in the original language about the history of those two adventurers who spoke in a language so close to their love. During study hours, they exchanged notes with jokes meant to alleviate their longing. The theme was, of course, the boy from another planet and the pilot lost in the desert. Tiquinho repeated the requests from the Little Prince and Abel responded with notes in return. "S'il vous plaît, dessine-moi un mouton," Tiquinho once wrote. Abel clumsily scribbled a sheep on the note and with no restraint in his role as the pilot wrote below it: "My little tiger, my little piece of Heaven."

And Tiquinho?

He locked himself in the bathroom, feeling like a real prince. And he wept with elation. Back outside, he carefully hid the note, which he would keep safe for a long time—long enough for the sheep's wool to turn yellow.

Didn't Tiquinho nurse delicious fantasies of love?

For example: being a vicar with Abel in the same parish, where they would live as celibates and saints, one for the other.

Didn't Tiquinho also have strange ideas about marriage?

Yes. He wanted to secretly marry Abel.

Forever?

Yes, because marriage was an indissoluble bond.

What did this mean, an indissoluble bond?

It meant that the union would only be broken when one of them died. It should be eternal, just as Saint John of the Cross wanted the union of the Soul with his Beloved, Jesus Christ, to be eternal.

And didn't the doctrinal aspect disturb Tiquinho?

Not then. If Tiquinho looked for explanations in the doctrine, it was only to live out his fantasies. He dreamed. He was delirious.

Did Tiquinho live outside of reason?

Tiquinho lived in a state of grace.

What was this state of grace like?

It meant being a Saint and dwelling in Paradise.

What, then, was Paradise?

Love and being loved by Abel. The beatitude of Paradise consisted in Abel's vision and in the possession of his love—for all eternity and for a life without end, as is desired in accordance with Christian doctrine, although we will see this would last less than a year. Oblivious to finitude, Tiquinho closed his eyes and supped the delights of the most tangible Heaven he had ever known. He felt no guilt. He had enormous energy for everything. It was the most fertile period in his formation.

Did Tiquinho levitate?

At least he felt that way: half a meter above the ground, due to Abel's love. His ecstatic moments in the chapel, though brief, were truthful. Lost in the contemplation of his tangible love, Tiquinho listened to the rumble of the imposing wings of the angels that surrounded him. He surrendered to murmurs that were as light as feathers caught by the wind, or brushing against each other. It was like hearing the delicate sound of his love. Tiquinho loved the angels.

Why?

Because on the side of men, angels were the most perfect beings that God created. Yes, there were those who rebelled against God and became evil angels. But this did not matter to Tiquinho; the others remained good angels.

Could Abel be considered a good angel?

Abel to him was the most fascinating of the good angels. Tiquinho, who liked to draw pictures of him with undulating wings, felt protected by his beauty and holiness.

What did Abel do when he learned he was a good angel?

He laughed, observing that he was the first pupil to become the angel of his own angel.

And Tiquinho, what did he answer?

That it was love between two angels, then. An angelic love, in other words.

Didn't Tiquinho once describe this love as something sacred in his diary?

Yes, in the same manner as he had answered the questionnaire—a formula that he would use many times, based on the model he had learned from Sister Elizabeth of the Trinity.

How did Jesus's love for Tiquinho come about in practice?

Jesus's love for Tiquinho would be like the love of the Spanish Gardener for Nicholas.

And how was the Spanish Gardener's love for Nicholas?

Just like the love between Tiquinho and Abel.

And how did the love between Tiquinho and Abel become manifest?

With affection, longing, and the exchanging of notes, gifts, and clothes. Sometimes there was a chaste kiss on the mouth. In general, their love was exchanged during the night.

Abel went to Tico's bed, and embraced him from behind—because "this is how you fit completely into my body." Tiquinho took refuge between Abel's bed sheets, resting his head on his chest, right where the shiny hairs flowed generously. But they didn't always lie down together. Tiquinho often preferred to sit on his knees beside Abel's bed, covering his face with kisses and telling him little love secrets. At other times, it was Abel who knelt in this exchange of veneration, calling him "my Tiquim" between clumsy kisses and long sighs of love. They lived a period of delicious courtship.

What did Tiquinho love most about Abel?

His gait of an unencumbered young lion. His eyes, whose brightness conveyed irresistible kindness. And of course, his sportsman's chest—not too wide, but spare, inviting, not arid, but softened by the black hairs of a Spanish gypsy.

Was Tiquinho fascinated by Abel's teenage body hair?

Abel's body hair delighted Tiquinho, because it manifested his virility with softness, a softness fragrant and matted in the armpits, but resplendent on the chest; yes, his greatest attribute was his resplendence. Tiquinho did not know Abel's pubic hair—he had not yet plunged so deep. But among the hairs offered for contemplation, those on his chest were beyond doubt what he craved on the horizon of his eye and heart. There he saw happiness, beauty, and peace stamped together. The meaning of these hairs went beyond the empire of the senses and pointed to the limits of mystery. For Tiquinho, so many revelations were hidden in that unpretentious patch of hair!

And Rachmaninov, how did it happen that he became part of their love?

One afternoon, in the Spiritual Director's room, Abel and Tiquinho accidentally discovered that album, whose cover explained how the author, discouraged by his first failures in front of the audience, could no longer compose and was then treated by a doctor who hypnotized him and told him over and over: "You are going to write a beautiful concerto." And Rachmaninov composed Concerto No. 2 for Piano and Orchestra. So, they both wanted to see how someone was convinced that he was capable of doing something beautiful. Listening to the concerto snuggled together, they realized that the doctor had achieved a real feat: it seemed to them that never before something so moving had been done in music. More than that, they were amazed that dozens of years later the doctor had led the Russian composer to perfectly express the indescribable love of two Brazilian boys. Hence, they listened to the same concerto innumerous times, together or separately, and relived those unfinished sensations of those who discover a realm for their own passion outside of themselves. Then, their love materialized into sounds, sometimes furious and sometimes sweet, coming from a piano in dialogue with an orchestra, in which tremendously subtle or explosively tempestuous chords were created by two interlocutors who were sometimes interpenetrated, and then again separated only to return, rolling almost dizzily, intersecting in an indissoluble manner in the beauty of the melody. Rachmaninov's insistent doctor became, in a way, a master of ceremony to their love. And Rachmaninov their prophet.

But didn't the Concerto sometimes make Tiquinho suffer?

Maybe because his fine sensitivity led him to pick up something premonitory in those sounds, Tiquinho felt his love blend with the tragic sensation of love's ending. But he also felt longing when Abel was not near. Then sometimes the Concerto was inevitably heavy-hearted. Perhaps he suffered from feeling that love inevitably contains a component of grief, when it goes too deep, reaching the membranes of pain. He realized at that point precisely that love is joy and suffering at the same time. When one loves too much.

It was said that Abel and Tiquinho exchanged their clothes?

Yes, when their sizes fit, which was not very common. They exchanged socks, handkerchiefs, and towels. As a game purely out of love.

In what other ways did this love become visible?

In so many others. Once, when he realized that Abel had not prepared himself properly for a school test, Tiquinho answered some questions wrong on purpose. That month, another student took first place in the class. Tiquinho and Abel stayed together—in second place. Another example: since he was still completely pious, Tiquinho offered Abel for his birthday an extraordinary Spiritual Bouquet that consisted of almost a hundred communions, fifteen indulgences (very difficult to obtain), two hundred different prayers, and more than a thousand sacrifices in Abel's honor.

And Abel?

Abel was less generous in his demonstrations of love. Nonetheless, he also let it show in furtive touches, little notes ("my tiny Tiquim"), and tender smiles that were like kisses sent through the air.

Didn't Tiquinho have visions of Abel?

Yes. He had visions of Abel even in the presence of Abel, who was transfigured into many things besides an Angel. On one of the communal walks to the beach, Tiquinho spent the day watching Abel's wet body. Abel loved the sea. Strangely, Tiquinho preferred to keep a distance, behaving as if he were a spy. He tracked the movements of Abel's muscles when he walked, ran, swam. He loved the form in which his wet shorts shaped Abel's crotch. He followed the descent of the salty water running down the back of his neck and spine. And he noticed the different forms in which the light shaped Abel's body, hour after hour. At dusk, he let himself be possessed by the image of Abel wrapped in unreal colors reflected by the sea. At that moment, both formed a single element. The water that had bathed Abel's body seemed to come off of him and Abel seemed to unfurl and become fluid, infinite, golden light to the horizon, sometimes interrupted by distant streaks of foam that undid this unreality made of pure gold. Tiquinho sat for a long time on a small dune, entranced by contemplation of the immeasurable volume of poetry created by his love. The Prefect of Discipline came to see if he was not ill. Tiquinho barely answered. He himself was unable to clearly see the potency of his visions. That afternoon, one might say that Abel was transfigured into sea itself. Therefore, Tiquinho loved the sea unconditionally.

Was Tiquinho forced to make many sacrifices for love?

In the Spiritual Bouquet he had given to Abel were included numerous sacrifices specifically for love. Since their courtship was becoming a favorite topic of conversation in the community, Abel and Tiquinho had to take some precautions that evidently affected Tiquinho, since he was targeted the most. He resolved to undertake an arduous plan to undo his fame as a sissy and "become a man" in the eyes of the community. The first measure was suggested and, let's say, imposed by Abel. Tiquinho needed to step away from the Flock, to which he, in the name of love, agreed. Although he had spared Canary as his confidant and friend, Tiquinho caused the end of the Flock, whose great days had already become a thing of the past—not least because Forpus's expulsion had already left the clique quite diminished. In any case, his relationship with Canary suffered from this compulsory separation and was thereafter never the same. Another measure—this one decided by Tiquinho himself— was to make an effort to participate more in sports and, doing so, to be identified less with the group of sissies. After three or four unsuccessful attempts at soccer, Tiquinho decided to dedicate himself to ping pong and volleyball— of course a sport associated with the most delicate boys. In any case, he tried so hard that he became a reasonably competent volleyball player. Out of love.

It seems that the need to "become a man" became an obsession for Tiquinho. Why?

The need had become more acute not only because of the rumors that circulated. At a certain moment, an old unease grew inside Tiquinho. If he had long feared that he was not a man like the others, some uncontrollable reactions in his body now began to accentuate this suspicion, which he evidently associated with a fear of sinning. Tiquinho had been getting increasingly pronounced erections with Abel. This took on such proportions that the mere thought of Abel reverberated, as if in a chain reaction, immediately between his legs, and terror took hold of Tiquinho. In addition to beginning to experience violent pains in his crotch due to a constant erection, an acute desire pierced his flesh and settled in a specific point of his body that began to manifest a persistent desire for Abel's priapic presence. Tiquinho suffered the same despair that Canary had felt for Log-Log. Because his desire for Abel's cock was relentless and more and more explicit, he wanted to keep it to himself, obstinately and entirely his own. He experienced a combination of attraction, curiosity, veneration, and necessity that was diabolically beyond his control and that sometimes hurt to the point that it was difficult for him to walk. He was ashamed to talk about it with Canary—as if he were looking for a cure with another convalescent. He tried to ask Father Marinho for advice. More than once he had been harshly warned against the harms of love for the flesh. When the Spiritual Director suggested that he should cut off relations with Abel, Tiquinho never sought his guidance again.

And Rachmaninov's Concerto No. 2—did it not help to appease these anxieties?

To the contrary. The Concerto had a quality of shaping and transforming itself along with the cadence of every new feeling of love. Listening to it became a torment. Tiquinho was writhing with pains in his stomach at the sometimes frenzied, then gelid merging and parting of the piano with the orchestra that Rachmaninov had just so suggestively arranged. The Concerto sounded like a heap of aching chords with no hope.

Did contradictions from then on begin to invade Tiquinho with ghosts and great fears?

Perhaps the contradictions in his mind were at least provisionally pacified. It was external circumstance that constantly added to these old contradictions renewed worries. In any case, these were opposites that he would have to face sooner or later. Indeed, sex began to emerge imperatively in Tiquinho's mystical fantasies. His despair grew with the approach of the holidays, which de facto decreed a separation from Abel for almost two months. Tiquinho thought of inviting him to stay at his house and then seducing him. He devised a plan: they would occupy beds next to each other, in his older brother's room, who would be out at the time; at night, Tiquinho would claim to be cold or lonely, and go to Abel's bed. There by themselves, there would be no prohibitions or regulations to stop him. He would surrender himself to Abel with all his passion. And he would see Abel naked for the first time, in one piece, his cock all naked, all its hair on display, precisely how he had wanted it every night. Tiquinho was truly disappointed when he extended the invitation and learned that Abel's parents would come and pick him up on the first day of vacation to take him home, far away. A week before they separated, Tiquinho was already experiencing pains of longing that would make his vacation hell.

What was the last questionnaire that Tiquinho answered, before leaving for the holidays without Abel?

With the anxiety of someone one who foresees disgrace approaching at a gallop, Tiquinho appealed to the carnal Jesus who lived in his fantasies, very manly, and completely like God. After Mass, on the day before he left for the holidays, he withdrew from the community immersed completely in packing bags and locked himself in a classroom, where he wrote two pages of his diary with allusive, exasperated, rebellious, and furiously desperate questions and answers that confronted the lacerating suspension of his love. My memory can still revive sparse and random bits.

How did Jesus live in Tiquinho?

Jesus lived in him through the Eucharist.

What was the Eucharist?

The Eucharist was the supreme encounter of love. This was when Jesus came to him with his blood flowing outside his body, and he went there and ate Jesus and licked and drank all the blood of Jesus. It looked like bread and wine, but it was truly the flesh and blood of Jesus that he swallowed.

What did the flesh and blood of Jesus taste like during this Act of love?

It allegedly tasted like a host and wine, as in the miracle. However, on closer attention one could taste the real blood and the real flesh.

Why did Jesus want Tiquinho to eat and drink him?

Because this is how one truly loves. One person is inside the other and they become one, in communion.

Did Jesus love Tiquinho too much?

His love was so large that Jesus wanted to stay inside Tiquinho.

So that was how one loved thyself according to Jesus's commandment in the Gospel?

Yes. One staying inside the other, as in a real miracle. That is why Tiquinho wanted to receive communion with Abel.

Of Desire in Fury

Which poem best describes this remembrance?

Perhaps an excerpt from Saint John of the Cross. Something like this:

> "Reveal your presence to me
> And kill me by your gaze and beauty
> See how the suffering
> Of love is only cured
> When you—or when your face—is near"
> —St. John of the Cross

Was this what Tiquinho felt, far away from Abel?

Yes. But he certainly didn't recite poems. He was desperate. During those almost two months of vacation, he woke up every night muttering the name of Abel, whom he saw everywhere. Abel's gleaming eyes, his gardener's face, the gypsy chest, the sportsman's thighs. And his sex? What would Abel's dick look like? Roundish, the balls? Wrinkled, the most hidden hairs? The world—all its questions and answers—was made of Abel. During his vacation Tiquinho barely left home. He tormented himself by scribbling letters to Abel.

Did he send him many?

He wrote them and tore them apart, one after the other. He feared the consequences.

Why was he afraid?

Because these were compromising letters in which he confessed his most visceral desire, his pains in the crotch, everything. He begged Abel to forgive him since he was destroying their friendship with his sin.

Did he never send any of these?

Yes, he sent one, halfway through the vacation. And he spent the other half of the holidays waiting for an answer that never came, much to his disquiet and anguish. He repeatedly looked under the door and even complained to the mail services, suspecting negligence, or an erroneous delivery address. Then he began to fear that his letter had provoked negative reactions in Abel. He had a dream in which he met Abel at the post office in his city. Abel was just about to send him a letter, but considering the coincidence, he preferred to deliver it personally; he smiled in a formal manner before turning his back and leaving without saying anything, accompanied by another boy, perhaps a rival.

And what was so serious about that letter?

In three or four lines, Tiquinho confessed to him his constant erection. Then, going straight to the point, he wrote something like this: "God gave me a fate, Abel. I love you like a woman. I want to be your wife." Period. He didn't think about anything else and ran to post it. Later, he was bitter with terror for what he had done.

Was Tiquinho right to fear so much?

Tiquinho feared the nature of Abel's love. In fact, fear was an essential component of his way of wanting Abel. In this case, he feared because he was secretly at a disadvantage.

Was it a real disadvantage?

Presumably yes. Tiquinho became aware of this whenever he measured the depth of his own feelings. For him, it was about loving Abel, or dying. In the face of such radicalism, Abel's feelings for him were at risk of being relegated to the background. Tiquinho knew, for example, that Abel had other vital interests—soccer, his playmates, maybe girls, vacation. He did not. He lived fundamentally immersed in

his inner world full of recesses. But he began to suspect—
without wanting to believe this—that their differences were
determined precisely by this feature: Abel's inner simplicity
meant that he was not compelled necessarily to merge affection and sex. Tiquinho saw this confirmed when, in a state
of distress that caused his eyes to jolt, he met Abel after
returning from vacation and felt in his gaze not that familiar spark of kindness, but a freshly lit crackle, something
skewed, unknown. He was fearful, yet unable to hide his
captivation, because the difference he sensed in his friend's
eyes transfixed him. Greed, he thought. Almost thirty years
later, one could say that this was the unmistakable proof of
erupting desire.

How could Tiquinho be sure of the difference?

After Abel confessed bluntly that he had often masturbated thinking of him during the holidays.

And Tiquinho's heart?

It leaped out of fear and delight.

So, Abel didn't find the letter strange?

No. Tiquinho's letter facilitated (or precipitated) what
Abel's gaze already foreshadowed. As soon as they recon-
nected, it was as if the lid was taken off of a boiling-hot cauldron. Each desired the other, body to body. Tiquinho over-

came his scruples—at least for now. They experimented with furtive touches, soon reaching deeper waters. They briefly met in the lavatories, where Abel displayed in full sight his unexplored regions. Tiquinho felt dizzy with a pleasure that was not exclusively his. The feline glow of Abel's eyes intensified, now shining in deep darkness. They signed up for the same shift to clean the dormitories. And it was with voluptuous joy that they together dipped the mop in the bucket and touched hands, delighted with soap and water.

And Saint Teresa's mad kisses, how did that work?

Lying in the same bed, at dawn they practiced the mad kisses of the *Song of Songs* and tasted all the delights that Saint Teresa too had imagined, having tasted them only in rare and ephemeral ecstasies.

Why call them mad kisses?

Because the boys' souls were out of control, exuberant with love.

Did they also feel they were dying of softness?

Sometimes of softness, sometimes of roughness. Because the joy that came from those touches was so excessive that their hearts lived in tumultuous agitation. Out of breath, they still separated only unwillingly. They went back to their own beds exhausted, wanting to dissolve even more.

In honor of Saint Teresa's kisses, Tiquinho again called Abel "my King."

And did they have orgasms?

More and more frequently. At first, when he exposed his cock, Abel acted with eagerness, hurriedly, and did not contain the flow of pleasure. Tiquinho went more slowly, with coyness, dripping almost. Until they caught up with each other. In time Abel slowed down, and Tico sped up.

Where did they have their meetings, besides the dormitory (at dawn) and the lavatory (furtively)?

That was the problem. They did extensive research to choose a place where they could be completely together. They started by going to the cellars in front of the storage rooms. Besides almost being discovered there once, by a Prefect who was especially fanatical about night surveillance, they were afraid of rats, spiders, and snakes. Despite cleaning the space and leaving a candle stub burning, they could not avoid these awkward intrusions. Often, while Tico and Abel kissed, rubbed, and breathed heavily, the rats ran by, squeaking and crashing into them. They definitively gave up on the basement that night when Abel almost stepped on a coral snake all ready to attack. Hence, they decided to opt for the outdoors. They started to make love to each other under the eucalyptus trees, where they took blankets, even though autumn ran late and the nights were still clear, warm. From then on, the eucalyptus trees became the favored place for their lovemaking, which started to merge with the strong scent of eucalyptus.

Didn't they grow tired of always interrupting their sleep?

Yes. Their tired eyes, thin appearance, and low grades were becoming evident. They lost their first place in class. Instead they got bags under their eyes. Anyone could see it.

And did Tiquinho's doctrinal concerns stop causing him qualms?

Temporarily, due to the insistence of Abel's sensuality, which dragged him into places soiled with love. Furthermore, such boldness was almost entirely new in Tiquinho's life. As long as this novelty persisted he could taste it without interference. Let's say he lived in a state of parentheses.

Then Abel took the lead in that love?

No doubt. The weird idea of the blood pact was his, for example.

Ah, the blood pact! Did it really exist or was it a figment of the imagination, created over time?

Putting together all the scraps of recollection, it is possible to claim with certainty that the blood pact existed as a true and terrible pact in which blood flowed and was exchanged. Abel was undoubtedly the leader who galloped ahead of the delirium.

How did this pact come about?

In an unoccupied moment of the day, inside the younger students' storage room, to which Abel had a key from a friend. They vowed eternal love, but now less with the mystical connotations of Tiquinho. It was done in a manner more to Abel's taste—practical, verifiable, direct. With a safety pin, each pierced the thumb of his own left hand. Abel sucked Tiquinho's pierced thumb and Tiquinho sucked Abel's pierced thumb, sealing the eternity of their love. Abel explained to Tiquinho that he had learned this in a film and warned him that it was a deadly serious oath, worse than swearing to God. In this case, they swore on each other's lives.

Did Tiquinho feel communion with Abel in that gesture?

No. This was not a real Eucharistic banquet, Tiquinho knew quite well. Once again, it was up to Abel to go ahead and propose communion in a more pragmatic, effective, full style: owning Tiquinho. He insisted in the name of love. And he insisted again, pleading with love. He caressed Tiquinho's back, in the light of the moon, and tried to prod him, enter him, calling him bittersweet names. Tiquinho struggled between holding back and opening up. There his religious anxieties reemerged, combined with moral scruples. Tiquinho began to feel his love with growing impatience. The more Abel wanted him, the more Tiquinho wanted Abel. And the more he resisted.

Were there specific reasons for this?

Humiliation, maybe. Already suffering from the stigma of the "sissies," Tiquinho feared the stigma of being a "faggot." And he feared this precisely in the name of love. Abel, on the other hand, continued to force his entry in the name of the continuity of love. Tiquinho cried, clinging to Abel's thighs, or sinking his head into the smooth hair on his chest.

Did this increase the difficulties between them?

Unquestionably. Abel's eyes shone in an increasingly fiery, inflexible way—and fiercely so, because they made commands in the name of a higher force unknown to both. Some of their amorous meetings resembled duels, in which one could imagine that, in the end, love's blood would flow between them.

How were these unusual duels?

Like this, for example: "Suck," ordered Abel. "No," whispered an insecure Tiquinho. "If you like me, then suck," insisted Abel.

Was it this argument that overpowered Tiquinho?

In many cases, yes. He longed to demonstrate the truth of his love. So, Abel won, although his contender shed no blood. Abel spilled the signs of his victory all over the little lover's face and mouth. Tiquinho, whose sense of smell and taste learned to delight in Abel's sperm, at heart believed he was privileged. But he felt the shadow of an uncertain biblical curse.

How did this dichotomy take shape in Tico's head?

It was the dichotomy between the male (Abel) and the female (Tiquinho), something that tortured him and filled him with resentment. For example, he feared, quite understandably, that Abel would stop loving him and would no longer respect him when he discovered that his friend was just a little fagot.

Was there anything else?

A lot more. At stake was the old and fearful sixth commandment.

And what things did the sixth commandment forbid?

Unfortunately, too many things. It was a cruel command because it didn't miss anything. It forbade acts, looks, words, and even unsuspecting thoughts against chastity.

And what was chastity?

Chastity was to abstain from Abel in thoughts, words, and deeds, which seemed impossible to the tormented Tiquinho.

Was it definitely out of the question for Father Marinho to help?

Definitely. Father Marinho could not deal with concrete facts. He was delirious in a much simpler way and he resolved his troubles by reading mystical texts, convinced by beautiful promises of eternity—as explained before. Abel and Tiquinho even began to avoid confessing to him, because they feared being expelled. They preferred the old confessor who came every fortnight; but still, they told him only half of their mortal sins.

Did this seem very grave to Tiquinho?

Extremely. Moral doubts were piling up like a ball of snow. In order to not arouse suspicions in the community, he saw himself forced to receive communion, despite his conviction that he was in mortal sin, which, according to the doctrine, meant a new mortal sin.

And Abel?

By that time, Abel already started to shrug his shoulders. He preferred to respond to concrete stimuli. Abstract things affected him increasingly less. His body overruled.

But wasn't the repression of his love ever more concrete?

That is true. Tiquinho and Abel's private friendship already formed part of the community's favorite gossip repertoire. Rumors spread about their nightly retreats. Often, even when they walked separately, this provoked whispers and jokes—too consistently not to disturb. On one occasion, Canary was pressured by one of the older students to report to the Prefect everything he knew about the "phenomenal couple"—as Abel and Tiquinho were sometimes called. Very uneasy and startled, Canary communicated this to Tiquinho, who warned Abel. This alarmed them. But the best they could do was keep their distance for a week, after which they started all over again, overcome by longing.

And then?

Then the situation reached a critical point, just at the end of Lent. The Rector called them both, separately. In addition to the accusation that they had withdrawn from community life and fallen behind in their studies, they were questioned about the insistent rumors, the details of which the Rector omitted, but not without insinuating them by rhetorical means. Tico and Abel denied the truth of what they most cherished in their lives. They were too terrified after the long interrogation and ensuing sermon. When leaving his office, the handsome Rector reminded them dryly that "private friendships will remain strictly prohibited in this house made for more noble ideals." And it was not a mere warning. Little before Palm Sunday, Tiquinho and Abel's beds were placed at opposite ends of the dormitory, right next to each of the Prefects of Discipline. The same happened with their desks in the study hall and in the classroom. Now, Abel and Tiquinho looked at each other from afar, across dozens of intercepting heads, in the atmosphere of agonizing Lent. They lived their love contortedly, trying to communicate with minimal glances. Each of their gestures was loaded with third and fourth meanings, which only they knew. Their communication became painful, dense, telegraphic. But their love was so contorted that it led directly back to its origins, where it again blossomed, as if by a miracle.

Under what stones did this miracle plant its roots?

Precisely under the cornerstone of Jesus's evangelical love, during Passion Week, so dear to Tiquinho. And it was on Holy Thursday that they not only rediscovered the meaning of their love, but acquired the strength to expand their passion to the limits of the possible.

Did that Holy Thursday leave indelible indications of mystery?

Yes. For Tiquinho and a large number of those boys, Holy Thursday inaugurated an atmosphere of transfiguration and made the Holy Week a mythical time. Palm Sunday brought to mind a mood of tragic premonition that would last until Wednesday, when the painful Office of Darkness was celebrated with fifteen candles, in a triangular chandelier, that were extinguished one by one to the sound of psalms and biblical lamentations, heightening their sorrow for the imminent death of Christ. But suddenly, in the midst of a divinity that was heavy with naked altars, with smoke of incense and purple cloths, the darkness would dissolve and Holy Thursday dawned like an interval of joy planted in the heart of death. Then they used white garments, covered the crucifix with a white linen cloth, sang Gloria again, played the organ, and festively rang the bells. That is, while they were commemorating his death, Christ was going to reveal the important message he had reserved for the final moment of his life. Holy Thursday commemorated the institution of love not only as a commandment, but as an anthropophagic devouring: at the Last Supper Christ had offered his body and his blood in the mystery of the Eucharist for anyone who wanted to love him to the point of full identification. Then he washed the disciples' feet, setting an example of what they should do for each other. It was with real delight that Tiquinho underwent the liturgical ceremonies: "In this I will recognize all those who are my disciples." If we love each other. He felt empowered, encouraged, redeemed.

Why was that year's Pediluvium particularly moving?

Because Abel took the place of one of the twelve apostles whose feet Father Marinho washed as an officiant. Abel was sitting right next to the altar, barefoot. During the ceremony, Tiquinho felt as close to Jesus as ever—physically close and spiritually identified. Abel's beauty radiated from his bare feet. For Tico, they were together, there at the altar, the One who had commanded to love and, in flesh and blood, the one who was loved in the name of such a commandment. The truth was revealed in front of his eyes as a complete, rounded, accomplished cycle. Suddenly, all barriers lifted between Abel's bare feet (which manifested their full nakedness) and the irresistible divinity that now enveloped them, as in a vortex. Everything came together.

How could the intensity of their love be interpreted during those moments of Holy Thursday?

This is impossible, because it would be necessary to know the language of trance. Only their spirits knew the secret formula to express this much fascination, which could not be talked about without choking on vain verbal attempts. Better, therefore, to keep those moments as memories of a legitimate inner mystery. There was indeed the rest: debatable external impressions that could be spilled into fragile metaphors. Like this one, for example: that afternoon, Abel seemed to have the same beauty as God.

And the beloved Saint John of the Cross, how did he come to share this very special moment of love?

Through Father Marinho, his spokesman. On the night of Holy Thursday, he performed the poem "Songs between the Soul and the Spouse," dramatized in the form of a one-act play, which the whole community attended in the chapel. The actors, dressed in a cassock and surplice, were divided into three groups: one interpreted the passionate Soul, another was the Beloved Spouse, and the last group were the Creatures. Tiquinho and Abel participated in the group of Creatures, which had few lines and played in the background of the presbytery. Hence, they had more time to pay attention to the beauty of the poem, which permeated them word by word, to the point of triggering the next events. The Soul, who had been struck by the arrow of the Love of God, chased the Beloved through the mountains and woods, and asked the Creatures to point her in the right direction, unaware that the Spouse was also seeking her, desperate for love. Until they met. Then the Soul surrendered to the Spouse in the caves and orchards, among pacified wild animals and birds that sang. In the quivering voices of the younger students who formed this group, the Soul thus clearly and openly stated its desire:

"Let us be happy, darling,
And see us mirrored in your beauty

On mountains and the hills
Where limpid waters plash
Let us go deeper in the wood."
—St. John of the Cross

Father Marinho, who had carefully instructed the children, wept during the performance. His dreams of beauty materialized the limits of inner feeling and were expressed in tears. For Tico and Abel, it was no longer a question of crying tears. All this love, ceaselessly celebrated and sung almost with exacerbation, gave urgency to this truly tangible immersion. Standing next to each other in the back of the group, they first grabbed hands and stayed like that, exchanging intense vibrations intent on overcoming, once again, the duality. They tried in vain: their two hands remained together. What could they do, but take a leap and cross the borders? This time, it was Tico who, perfectly possessed by the love of God, accepted the challenge. His ears brimming with Saint John's amorous cooing, Tiquinho freed his hand and slowly, like someone who never is, nor was afraid, tucked it in the pocket of Abel's cassock and groped until he found his cock—the flesh already rigid, perfectly sensitive to the call of that beatific day. Someone offered. Someone took possession of the rediscovered treasure.

And what did Tiquinho do in this trance?

Initially, he touched it lightly, because the sacred jewel at first intimidated him. Then he wanted more palpable knowledge. He squeezed. And to test the treasure's identity, he tightly grabbed a hold. Then he took possession of what he felt naturally belonged to him. And there he remained, as someone who had finally reached the beginning of everything.

Does memory register sensations?

Yes, scattered ones. Fragments of dizziness and almost-spasms of delight. Abel responded by grabbing the hand that held him. It was a gesture by one who sensed that, from then on, there was no going back. Nor did John of the Cross's baroque generosity cease to encourage him.

What events followed from this?

As was said, the daily rhythm of the Seminary was entirely disturbed, and the whole community began holding nightly turns, rotating groups for the Adoration of the Eucharist, or the Vigil of the sacrificed Christ. Tico and Abel took advantage of this period overflowing with sanctity, and fled.

In this case, wouldn't their escape be transfiguration?

Yes. Leaving the community's collective transfer of souls behind, they undertook a crossing-over in a rapturous flight

directed toward their own bodies. During the three holi-
est nights of Passion Week, the infirmary turned into their
Promised Land.

And how did this flight, which was a journey, or a meeting, occur?
Abel entered the infirmary and was completely naked. He
left his cock exposed, unafraid to reveal his desire in its pul-
sating stiffness. Tico could no longer resist and did what he
had longed to dare. Abel took his communion, to the last
drop of blood.

So it was no longer a communion without bloodshed?
No. Tiquinho completely sucked it in, but he did bleed
during the three nights they were together. These were cuts
of love, their own love, a love in which both were fiercely
chained together, awed by the sensation of eucharistic
devouring.

*Do you mean that blood of love finally flowed in the duel between
them?*
The duel no longer mattered. There certainly was blood.
And Tiquinho wanted more. And insatiable was their desire
to share communion till nothing would be left of him or the
other. On each of those sacrosanct nights, Abel delighted
in showing off his naked body, as if to signal the beginning
of their ritual. And Tiquinho, the worshiper, with shooting

eyes collected himself to engage and fervently repeat the secular gesture of two becoming one.

How long did this apogee of mystical and carnal idyll last?

The time of the Resurrection. Their love blazed so brightly that it seemed to push the limits of the possible. But no. Unquestionably rigid, the boundaries of the possible had only temporarily been lifted in the excessive atmosphere of religious sanctity. This resurrection lasted only three days and its fleetingness can never be sufficiently lamented.

What happened next?

Next, the demon stuck its claws in the realm of passion. In this case, the demon certainly did not feel like an abstract entity.

What, then, was the demon?

Perhaps it was the dark side of passion. But it could be other things. Even prosaic, fragile reasons crystallized in daily life and lodged in the heart of beauty: doubts, fears, wear and tear, teenage angst. Many call this poison of unclear composition "demon." That is why it is legitimate to say that the devil spread his wings like an evil angel. And there, he established the horrendous limits of the possible in the form of sin.

What was sin?

Sin was to love God above all things, and to love Abel above God. Tiquinho would not be the same after discovering this notion.

Of Crying and Grinding Teeth

Was the final hour of their love sad?
Tiquinho found it sad and terrifying.

How was its ending announced?
In signs that Tiquinho accidentally began to pick up. For example, he sensed and anticipated the intricate overtones of the ending in a new album that Father Marinho acquired at the time. Listening to music was in fact one of the few activities in which Tiquinho still gladly took part. He went to the Spiritual Director's room to immerse himself in the peculiar chants of the *Carmina Burana*, which for him combined perversity, loneliness, and magic in a unique and inextricable manner. Sitting in his corner, he surrendered to the invasion of drunken chords that come from another world and that pointed to an eschatological time, when there would be no trumpets, but only crying and gnashing of teeth. His vision of the apocalypse was announced with those pagan cymbals and drums.

Were there any nightmares at the end?

Yes. Nightmares that Tiquinho started having right after the celebration of the Resurrection. The arrival of his love's final hour was preceded by furry animals, thousands of disgusting creatures, as far as the eye could see. Not only rats. Wings of bats whirring past. And spikes stabbing sinners according to their sins. Complaints, mocking voices that modulated into macabre, absurd sounds. And gaping devouring mouths. And blood coming out of the place where feces should be. Misleading celestial cymbals that introduced hissing demons with long nails and an immense sex ejaculating purulent spit. But also, an immense phallic antler. Or else, a plain of apparent beauty, which became horrifying when revealed up close: human beings with wounds all over their bodies, four eyes, a wart in the place of their nose, while drums beating for no reason made senseless noises on earth.

And snakes, were there slimy snakes?

Many. Many snakes coiling up to the sound of the cymbals, slithering in treacherous tranquility and curling around him almost tickling, and then starting to pressure the vertebrae, with high-pitched, melodic screams. And severed heads, dancing to the sound of the choirs, cymbals, and drums of the pagan *Carmina*. Tiquinho woke up suffocating with terror.

Were there also nightmares when he was awake?

Yes. Tiquinho began to become obsessed with the nakedness of Jesus.

Would he think, for example, of Christ's sex?

Yes. Jesus's sex and Abel's cock were the same thing: a pink flower encased by black, fragrant hairs, moistened with sweat. Tiquinho saw him enveloped in majesty, light, and bloody sperm of Redemption. He could not avoid these delectable visions that filled him with fear and compunction.

Did he fear that he could not become a priest?

Yes. He had learned that one of the telling signs of the elect's calling was purity and non-recurrence in mortal sin. In addition to fearing the sixth commandment, he judged himself too attached to earthly things—to the world, which increasingly meant Abel.

Did Tico return to mystical contemplation as an attempt at sanctification?

Yes. But this time he contemplated with mortification and guilt. He spent hours in the chapel, in worship of the crucified Christ. His delight in nakedness merged with the almost physical nearness of Jesus's suffering.

Did he suffer with Christ?

Tiquinho bore his sadness and pain on the cross. He drew back on a bench in the chapel and felt his wounds throbbing and burning with sharp, fierce pangs. This was his way of consoling himself. Since he knew that the mystery of Redemption lay in the Passion and Death of Christ, he wanted to suffer in order to save the world. In fact, he himself hoped to redeem himself before Christ. Such a disposition would not have caused particular concern, were it not that Tiquinho was found one afternoon yelping like an animal. With a helpless and pleading look towards the image of the Crucified, he whined softly in the chapel. The Spiritual Director called him and posed questions. Tico listened. He had nothing to answer.

And Abel?

Abel was embarrassed, alarmed, and insecure in the face of such a situation. He shouted at Tiquinho and called him weak during a volleyball game in which they played on the same team and lost. Pure nervousness.

Was it not very painful for Tico to hear that from Abel's mouth?

It was an indescribable pain. Also, because he therein saw proof of Abel's subtle detachment, without managing to understand why. It seems that it was a vicious circle: the further Abel removed himself, afraid of Tico's unhealthy symptoms, the stranger and more taciturn Tiquinho became. He was no longer seen in the playgrounds. He isolated himself in the study hall, or in the chapel, and during communal activities, such as music recitals or cleaning jobs, he was lost in thought. His academic performance dropped noticeably, in such a manner that everyone bore witness to the end.

And the superiors?

The Rector called him to ask about his health. He ended up recommending a fortifier that was available in the infirmary. It was shortly thereafter that Tiquinho started experiencing severe headaches. He consulted the doctor, who prescribed a tranquilizer. But the headache persisted. Terrified, Tiquinho confided to Abel that he had brain cancer. And he repeated this story exhaustively to several friends. One day he passed out during the afternoon recess. The priests decided that he was suffering from a nervous breakdown and thought it best to send him home, where he would rest for a couple of weeks.

Did Tiquinho rest?

Tiquinho couldn't bear his longing for Abel. Four days later, he was back at the Seminary by his own decision and to everyone's surprise. He swore to the Rector that he felt perfectly well. And he ran to find Abel.

What was the big surprise, then?

Abel was in the locker room creating an uproar with a group of players after a soccer match, and he didn't even seem to notice Tiquinho's entrance. He took off his soccer shoes and socks, complained about some poor passes. Nothing more. Tiquinho came closer—enough to taste the scent of fresh sweat—and murmured a hello. To his bewilderment, Abel turned around and continued laughing at someone on the opposite side. Tiquinho remained static for a few seconds, refusing to admit it. He only came to himself when silence invaded the locker room. Everyone had withdrawn, including Abel, who had not given him a single look of love. Tico ran after them, reached the group that was headed for the lavatories, approached Abel and stared him down with an unexpected hatefulness that had suddenly began to well up from nowhere. Only then did Abel look at him and mumble a hello so banal that it would have been better to have just remained silent.

What thought occurred to Tiquinho, in the midst of his hate?

This: You become forever responsible for what you have tamed. But Abel no longer seemed responsible for Tiquinho. The fox had been wrong.

Did Tiquinho understand what had happened?

He suspected that he had become repulsive to Abel. But he didn't feel the need to ask more. His fury and jealousy emerged so brutally that he demanded no explanation: ever since that moment, little João Tico-Tico became a creature overflowing with murderous desires. For the next few days, he observed Abel from afar—an increasingly carefree Abel—and felt a resentment build up that filled him with unknown intensity. He watched silently, taking his time. He intended his wrath to be divine.

Had Abel changed from a good angel to a rebel?

No doubt. Tiquinho felt betrayed. Abel seemed a bad angel who had rebelled against his love, out of pure venality.

Did he desire to punish this rebellious angel?

From then on, Tiquinho was completely invested in the task of revenge. The love they had shared was too radical to be lost without an opposite reaction of equal intensity. He wanted to punish fiercely, calculatedly. Like an uncompromising and cunning God.

What punishment did rebellious angels deserve?

They deserved to be expelled from heaven and condemned to hell. This, Tiquinho had decided. He merely had to wait for the right opportunity.

And when did this opportunity arise?

Almost a week later. The Rector was absent due to an illness in his family. Precisely one of those nights, there was no light shortly before bedtime. The students' rioting started in the study hall, where in the dark some were beginning to tap their fingers on the lids of their desks, and extended to the dormitory, where it turned widespread and so, finally, into a riot. No one paid attention to the threats and vain warnings from the Prefects of Discipline, which were barely audible in the confusion. Father Marinho also tried to intervene, but the students had never taken him seriously in matters of discipline. When someone discovered that in their part of the city everything was dark—perhaps because of a defect somewhere in a power transformer— the students felt even more at liberty, and the turmoil then almost tuned into mutiny. The seminarians screamed and ran through the manor, slamming doors and windows. Many turned their attention to the lavatories, turning on all the taps and splashing each other with water. Demonic figures were seen running across the outer courtyard, leaving an echo of shrill screams. Even the nuns came out of their quarters, like little animals scared and perplexed by the strange events. The dormitory of the oldest students had become the scene of a wild feast. For no apparent reason, someone decided to undress. That was the tipping point. Within a few minutes, naked bodies ran between the beds, or jumped on the mattresses, as in a circus. One of the Prefects appeared with a flashlight that was quickly confiscated and integrated in the game, so that, from then on, a playful spotlight accompanied the improvised parade of naked bodies, illuminating their private parts. That unthinkable spectacle in an institution where the Lord's elect was instructed is forever seared in my memory. Their bodies were like an obscene will-o'-the-wisp: buttocks were illuminated, pointing at onlookers, and then suddenly dissolved in the darkness. Fleeting cocks were swinging to the rhythm of demonic leaps, if not already handled provocatively and lasciviously, amid the roars and applause of the spectators. As a precaution, their faces were not lit, and if they inadvertently entered the light they hid behind their arms, or were covered by pillows. When the second Prefect of Discipline came out with another flashlight, Tiquinho, until then not involved, had a dexterous, uncontrollable impulse. In keeping with the general madness, he took possession of the flashlight and took its bright spotlight through the entire bedroom in search of Abel, whom he had recognized among the naked bodies. It did not take long to locate him on a bed, right in the center of the bedroom, jumping up down and swirling around to better show off his beauty. Tiquinho felt in his throat that the moment of revenge had arrived. Smiling with secret pleasure, he not only fixed the beam on Abel's naked body and face, but pursued him when Abel attempted to flee. The crowd's attention was then concentrated on that duel of light and shadow, in which everyone could verify the beauty of Abel Rebebel's ass and of its strikingly black hairs. Clinging to the flashlight, Tiquinho was relentless like an enraged rival in a melodramatic movie. Enveloped by dark shadows, one might say that he had the stony face of a perfectly bad actress. And it was in that instant that he heard the perverse chords of the *Carmina Burana* again, as if choirs of mocking voices and giggles obscenely mixed with cymbals and drums that came out of the depths of his soul, puking hatred and spewing an almost volcanic evil. Abel tried to hide and nervously began putting on his pajamas, since the spotlight refused to leave him. This only made it worse: everyone witnessed that Abel Rebebel, after he was cornered and revealed, launched into a fierce, evil, humiliating fight. Tiquinho felt as righteous as the guardian of the gates of Paradise, carrying his flaming sword. After the riot was over, he still pointed the light directly at Abel's imploring face. When the Prefect of Discipline took back the flashlight from his hands, Tico could still taste the strong flavor of revenge, which, once activated, he had intention of stopping.

Did it stop?

No. With ardent hatred that continued to shroud his love, Tiquinho's revenge went on as planned.

And how did his plans come about?

Upon his return, the Rector brought the Prefects together in the study hall and for an hour spewed his wrath on those mute and livid faces. Considering the seriousness of the incident, which, in addition to betraying his trust, was unworthy of young men elected to the priestly ministry, he promised the strictest possible punishment. Before retiring dramatically, he demanded in a roaring voice that the culprits be identified. An uncomfortable silence came over the study hall. Seconds later, the silence was broken by three dragging chairs. The two Prefects and Tiquinho got up and went straight to the Rector's office.

Wouldn't Tiquinho, by doing so, accelerate the final hour of love?

No. The final hour is part of the mystery of passion. As for Tiquinho, he was completely beside himself. His overflowing love led him to the Rector, to reveal Abel's nakedness, thus confirming reports made by the Prefects. On the same day his vengeance was fulfilled. Abel was called in by the Rector, who informed him of his immediate removal from the Seminary.

Was Tiquinho satisfied?

How could he? He washed away all his hatefulness and placated his demons. But he found the opposite of peace, when faced with the curse of an unbearable truth.

What truth would be so terrible at that moment?

The most obvious: Abel was not guilty, and Tiquinho from now on could no longer admire the image of Abel. With his vengeance complete, there remained a vista of irremediable ruins and pure wreckage inside Tiquinho's heart. So came the moment of remorse. Tiquinho spent two sleepless nights, terrorized by guilt. He felt eternally responsible for the one he had tamed.

And Abel?

Abel went into a regime of complete isolation the next few days, while he waited for his parents to arrive and pick him up. Since he was no longer considered a seminarian, he was to remain entirely outside of the community's daily life, eating after all the others, and living in a guest room. Likewise, it was forbidden for students to communicate with him, or even approach him.

What other events followed towards the end?

Some students were expressly punished, and the whole community suffered from the suspension of various liberties. But after the initial shock, Abel's expulsion became part of the routine, like a crime that deserves punishment. It is true that many regretted the loss that their soccer team had suffered. But that was it. In those last days, Tiquinho suffered an atrocious loneliness. From the bottom of his guts he felt a need to speak to Abel, before the irreversible outcome.

Why did he need to talk to Abel so badly?

Because he suffered various modalities of pain that only Abel could alleviate. He wanted to murder him, yet also ask him forgiveness a thousand times. He wanted to declare himself in love, a slave, and a wife for all eternity. He wanted to start over in whatever manner that Abel preferred, and to see this moment as only a short interval. And if his departure were really inevitable, Tiquinho needed Abel to bless him, as the Angel did with Jacob after the fight. He suspected—and this made him suffer even more—that the Angel was going to leave in silence, perhaps because both contenders were defeated. These suspicions made Tiquinho feel lost in the world. Without Abel, he would turn into a miserably helpless being.

Did Tico try to breach the prohibition of communication with Abel's?

He tried to communicate with Abel in several ways. He prowled around the guest rooms, trying to visit him, repeatedly and at different times, including at night. But each time he was intercepted by the invigilating Prefects. Then he passed his time following Abel's figure from afar, and his heart sank when he saw him go alone to the cafeteria, outside the communal schedule. The basement had become his main hideout and observation post. It was from there that he monitored the distant movements of his expulsed gardener.

How did Tiquinho foresee Abel's absence?

Like a vision of hell, where he would suffer eternal fire and indescribable evils.

What kind of terrible evils?

All this could be summarized with his deprivation of Abel, because his absence was equivalent to death, and his disappearance was equivalent to nothingness, since Abel was everything. That is why Tiquinho, hiding out in the basement, began concocting desperate plots.

What kind of plots?

Abel's death and his own simultaneous suicide. He tended mostly towards fire: he would set Abel's room on fire and die with him. Finally, he opted to spend a night in the cold rain of late autumn. And so he did, standing in the middle of the soccer field. There, drenched in despair, he wished to catch pneumonia to die of love—as in old dramas, perhaps.

And the fateful day, when did it arrive?

On the same morning of his suicide attempt, Tiquinho

noticed suspicious movements near the guest rooms. He ran to the visiting room and saw an old couple waiting heavy-heartedly. He hurried back to the basement and, with eyes glowing in the dark, managed to still see the Spanish Gardener leave with the same old suitcases, escorted by the Rector and the two Prefects in charge of the older students. Tiquinho reviewed the familiar scene: Abel would try to escape and end up dying by the police bullets, out of love for his boy. Then, the film seemed to him too cruel, precisely because he was the one left behind—little Nicholas and the Little Prince, incurably thrown back to their lonesome planet.

Did Tiquinho cry?

The time for beneficent tears was over. This time he could only cry tears that saddened him even more. That time was more conducive to rebuking and grinding teeth.

What did he do then?

He ran to the study hall, picked up the notebooks of his diary, and hid in the eucalyptus grove, where he stayed crouched for a long time, trying to convince himself that Abel was really gone. Then he tore up the notebooks, made a mound with dry leaves and set everything on fire. From there, he ran to the basement, where he started banging his head against the wall, shouting Abel's name, violently.

And how did this become a troubled day for everyone?

At night, the eucalyptus trees were in flames, creating shimmers of the apocalypse in the gray sky. There was a great stir at the seminary, with the students grazing the edges of the eucalyptus trees to isolate the fire, and running chaotically with containers of water that came and went. The soccer field became a circle entirely enveloped by flames, a blazing inferno where young lovers once had wanted to move mountains. When the firefighters arrived, there was little to do, not least because a thin rain was already falling. The next morning revealed a landscape now austere and forlorn: the naked soccer field, and around it, tree trunks, blackened and still smoking. A heap of bones in a cemetery.

And Tiquinho?

He didn't see any of this. That same morning, he was found unconscious in the basement. His head was cut and his hair was caked with clotted blood. They took him to the infirmary, where he was medicated and only woke up at night, with a terrible headache. After that, he did not utter a single word. He spent two days with bewildered eyes, refusing to eat or sleep. One night, one of the Prefects found him wandering around the outside courtyard, in his pajamas and with a bandaged head. Father Marinho went to visit him. Even though he knew the source of his sufferings, he did not dare tread there. He asked banal questions, attempted some consoling phrases, made him drink some milk. Tiquinho remained mute. Minutes later, he threw up the milk in short, silent spasms. In the afternoon of the following day, the nurse found him shaking with violent tremors all over his body, like a demon. She also discovered the bed had been wetted. The Rector worried about the news and sent for a doctor who diagnosed a state of precoma. Tiquinho was rushed to the hospital, where he stayed for a few days, until he recovered. From there, they took him directly to his parents' house, where he spent weeks on bedrest, taking injections of vitamins and sleeping pills, since his insomnia was persistent. He never returned to the seminary.

What was his last memory of this disturbed farewell?

On the stretcher, while crossing the central hallway towards the ambulance, Tiquinho had the vague impression of hearing the sound of bells. They seemed like the distant bells of the Angelus, but Tiquinho never knew for sure. That was his very last memory of those days.

Missa Est

I SUDDENLY wake up from a dream. But these are not the chimes of the Angelus. They seem to be tolling for the morning mass. The light outside floods the room. In front of me, the flowered skull has lost its magic. I see only a tasteless vase in enameled ceramic of a nondescript green color. The lilies look defeated by the weight of a sleepless night and now exude a tired scent.

As I wash my face in the adjoining bathroom, it occurs to me that, many years ago, Abel was banished to one of these rooms, perhaps the same one I now occupy. Who knows what he thought, what he suffered, how he hated. I look at myself in the mirror. In front of me stands a Tiquinho with markings of time around his misty eyes, on his drooping cheeks, and in the furrows that are beginning to take over the entire area of his face. An anesthetized being.

❖ ❖ ❖

I leaf through Saint Teresa. O life, life! How can you bear to be absent from that which is your life?

What does God refer to, what are these exclamations, what love can be on fire like this? I ask my double.

I face the outside. The sun shines, outlining the same symmetrical shadows as thirty years ago. I walk to the inner courtyard. Where there once was a delicate garden, now I find holes in parched earth. Remains of flower beds. Abandoned plants. Some loose shrubs.

The orphans arrive, walking in line. They are younger than I thought. On their way to the cafeteria, watched by two lay brothers, they pass me in silence. I sense that each of them registers my presence in detail. They keep their heads turned towards me as they pass. Some even look back, firmly. They don't smile, but their eyes glisten. There is something dangerous in their manner, as if they covet me and want to take immediate possession. I feel an indeterminate, but lacerating aggressiveness in the air. Tremors run through my body.

I wander aimlessly through the outer courtyard. I caress the bricks of the ugly columns. They are eaten by time and in many places darkened. In vain I try to feel the past through touch.

❖ ❖ ❖

I walk among the eucalyptus trees. The trees are tall and green. But I have the impression of seeing scorched spots on some trunks, and remains of blackness on trunks that lie in the grass. A total illusion, I think. In all these years, the eucalyptus grove has completely recovered.

❖ ❖ ❖

As I return to the courtyard, the orphans are just coming out of the cafeteria, as always, in line. As soon as one of the priests blows a whistle, they turn into boisterous machines and come running towards me, like a swarm. In a few seconds, I'm surrounded by children who entrap me. I find myself trying to smile like a compassionate adult. I am jostled on all sides. They elbow each other and compete for me, and hold out their impatient or imploring hands to me: "Pick me up!" I lift one of them. His joy does not take the form of a smile. On his little face, I see instead a frightened frown, combined with a delight that makes him breathless. I am horrified. The child wants to scream with pleasure, but cannot. When I put him back on the ground, I am attacked by dozens of fierce claws. I pick one up, and another, and again another. There high up, they all give a glimpse of the same joyous intimation that leaves their mouth bizarrely wide-open and takes their breath away when I hold them. Some are not satisfied and want me to repeat it. I notice that they are becoming more aggressive. They fight each other, and compete for a moment of my time, for a piece of me. I continue my task, unsure whether I am moved or want to cry out in terror. I lift another and put some more on my lap, always forcefully pushed and pulled about.

I feel that my shirt has been torn in the back, and that five nails are digging in to possess me. I start to fear those eyes gleaming with desire, those outstretched arms, and the screams emitted almost mindlessly: "Now me!" "What about me?" "Take me!" "I want it too!" Some already cry, are trampled down. When I realize that I am the banquet here, I panic. Just when I am about to scream, I am saved by one of the priests who had been making his way towards me.

What did he say? What did I hear, right here in my ear? An unconscious slip, or a delusion of the imagination, I say to myself. And just like that, some verses of Saint Teresa come to mind: My beloved is for me and I am for my beloved. These are the first words that occur to me, before I ask myself again: Who would come looking for me in this place?

Abel Rebebel, the priest repeats, in a neutral manner.

I think of saying that Abel does not know of my return. But I notice the ridiculousness of my observation in time. Instead, I throw open my mouth, trying to ask, Where? But I don't know if I would rather know, Why? Or even more, How? What is certain is that I stumble over my questions: That Abel?

❖ ❖ ❖

In the visiting room. Someone awaits. He introduces himself as Abel Rebebel.

❖ ❖ ❖

Suddenly, I return. Like someone crashing down, I contemplate myself from a distance. I see my double reflected in the big mirror of a world where the reverse of this appearance, taken too seriously for too long, takes place. I no longer argue: at the entrance, a certain Spanish Gardener is waiting for me. I think without hesitation about troubling my other self: Abel is here, after so many years. Abel, was our pact really that serious?

The children have moved away. Now they scream, have scattered around the outer courtyard, and, while my inner world is mirrored in the objective landscape, I pause, musing on my doubts: Would Abel have returned after so long? Or was he waiting for me all these years at the gates of Heaven, my dear Abel? Who arranged this meeting? Why? Suddenly, I shudder, already lost in my delusion. It doesn't matter, whether Abel came back or waited obstinately. The truth is that he came to avenge himself. In the visiting room, a terrible punishment awaits me. Not to wound with love, but to launch a revenge attack against the one who betrayed him. I try to defend myself against my double. I try to gather arguments in favor of my love. I remind him how I too suffered, given that I was also rejected. I want to prepare myself to convince Abel that I am not guilty.

The priest taps me on the shoulder and insists. In the visiting room, there he is, waiting. I realize I haven't even moved.

I pronounce his name as if it were a magical invocation, and I hear reverberations that are perhaps part of a delusion. Then I start walking towards Abel, or whoever was waiting for me there. There are voices, many pressing voices. Half of me is afraid. The other half loves to fear Abel. During this stroll.

During this stroll, something bygone brings me back to consciousness. Although I stumble, I find myself crossing the courtyard, bent over by doubts that leave me restless like a young virgin on her way to the wedding room. Am I really going to find Abel down the hall?

I glide even further into the well, into this new reality that has become a mirror. There are incubi that watch over me, little ones. There are mystical, invasive, confused memories. It seems I am praying, because the passion is hurting me again. From the depths of my clamoring being, new pagans contrive sanctified, evangelical, and delirious verses of love that become mine. I, who do not know who I am, who strives for nothing more, because I, being absent from you, what life can I live?

Father, tell Abel to wait—I hear myself saying.

I want to prepare, make myself handsome. But there is no time. Afflicted, I cry out to the night, O night that guided me, night sweeter than dawn, night that joins loves, now transform one into the other, O transfigured night. Why? I have no business whatsoever. My task is to love.

I hurry, unsure whether I'm not crazy. What weapons will Abel's love use? With what caresses will it annihilate me? Why did he hide for so long, leaving me to groan after he wounded me?

When I am climbing the stairs at the end of the courtyard, I notice that my terrified love shines and flickers, not like an oil lamp, but like an apocalyptic torch. I feel behind me something that insinuates hell, too close, too hot. Or would

I have internalized the flames of eternity? I see my double looking sideways. And I almost lose my breath when I foresee that my inner hell comes from outside. So, I force myself not to resist: when my feet reach the top of the stairs, I force myself to take courage, and turn my face backwards in the direction of the courtyard. There is no hell at all, but only pure celebration. My skin burns in the reflection of shooting flames, so real that they look like steel plates piercing the eyes of what I am, there, astonished and in love. Twenty-five years later, the eucalyptus trees burn again, forming a circle of fire around the soccer field. I, somewhere between shaken and fascinated, feel my legs falter and the one supporting my body almost collapses. Amid the flare of the flames, the orphans run disorderly, perhaps in flight, perhaps possessed by the same love that invades every particle in the air, breaking down barriers, undoing history, distorting fate. I hear whistling, bells, and screams that pierce like human cymbals. I pay attention to what my ears gradually start to make out: in unison, the voices repeat the same spellbinding formula that subverts everything. I join in with the choir. I hear my own sound moving away, calling. And I receive it back, this cry that comes out of who I am, without knowing which one.

Abel. Abel Rebebel.

I have the impression of being at the center of an ancestral celebration. And these repetitions of the same name, they sound like articulate prayers. I hear myself begging for mercy, because I cannot endure this much love, and I see my body almost running, moved by the name of Abel, which wells up from some mysterious point in the depths of me, or from outer space. Life, don't be burdensome, I then think with supreme courage. Remember that you have only to lose yourself in order to win. Come now, oh sweet death, do not delay in arriving, that I die, because I do not die. If I am going to die of love, then I must hurry.

I am the one who hurls himself towards the entrance, a product of pure passion. I am going to meet an angel with big undulating wings, outside of Paradise. Whether as Avenger of Love, or as Everlasting Spouse, it doesn't matter. Now we are interchangeable.

I will soon reach my secret center.

WARNING

The author asks the readers for forgiveness, and confesses not knowing the outcome of this drama.

Uncertainties of fiction? Weakness of memory, perhaps.

Paulicéia/ Maurícia/ Filipéia,
April/ August of the year of grace 1982.

About the Author

JOÃO SILVÉRIO Trevisan is arguably one of the most important LGBTQAI+ activists in Brazil. Since his first novel in the 1960s, he has addressed same-sex desire and discussed important questions for the queer community. He created, alongside other prominent figures, the first gay newspaper in 1978, *Lampião da esquina*. He was also a member of Somos, one of the very first gay organizations in Brazil. Consequently, he was at the forefront of the first responses to the AIDS crisis in Brazil in the early 1980s. His career spans throughout the past five decades in literature, essay, cinema, activism, and journalism.

His first movie, *Orgia ou homem que deu cria*, now a cult classic, was one of the first to address queer desire on screen. His latest books are *Pai*, a memoir recounting the troubled relationship with his father and, most recently, *Seis balas num buraco só*, a very provocative book of essays discussing masculinity and its effects on our society.

About the Translators

BEN DE WITTE (he, ele, él) holds a doctorate in comparative literature from Rutgers University and currently teaches courses in literary studies and translation at the University of Leuven. Ben has published scholarly articles and review essays in the area of modern drama and performance, queer modernism, and translation studies.

JOÃO NEMI NETO (he, ele, él). Brazil. João is a writer, translator, and teacher. His first novel, *Os dois piores anos da minha vida*, came out in 2021. It is a young adult story regarding his coming out as a teenager in the countryside of Brazil. His first book of poetry, *Corpo(s)*, was published in São Paulo in 2016. He collaborated with a collective of Latin American writers for *The US without us* (Sangria Editores 2015), published in New York and Santiago, Chile; and *Tente Entender o que tento dizer. Poesia: HIV/AIDS* organized by the poet Ramon Nunes Melo in 2019. His latest book is *Cannibalizing Queer: Brazilian Cinema from 1970 to 2015* (Wayne State UP 2022).

Printed in the USA
CPSIA information can be obtained
at www.ICGtesting.com
JSHW081002091123
51784JS00001B/2